Other books by Sherrie DeMorrow:

Knight and Daye
Cloud of Dreams
The Elder Rose
All The Land
The Little Bird

THE LITTLE BIRD

BY

SHERRIE DEMORROW

Published 2018 by

Lightning Source (UK) Ltd
Chapter House,
Pitfield,
Kiln Farm,
Milton Keynes
MK11 3LW,
UK

Cover Art Design by Sam Wall

To LL for help and support

To the memories of LH, GP, JH, DN, IC, and especially AC,

who continues to inspire my work

PREFACE

Please note **this is a book of fiction** and **NOT** meant as an accurate representation of historical events. The reader must suspend all preconceptions of belief in past history. There may be some reality in detail to it, but most of the scenarios are FAKE.

The historical attitudes towards sensitive issues, and people's prejudices of the time, had to remain intact to provide a sense of realism in the story.

Some place names given are **NOT** real, unless otherwise stated or recognised as real. Other characters (for the most part) are fictional and loosely based on people known of by the author.

CHAPTER I

The province of Britannia was one of the farthest outposts of the Empire. It was, indeed, a *damp nation*, yet not damp in spirit. Over the years, slaves from these far reaches had come to serve the Empire, within its many conquered lands. Tribes were subdued, families left behind in the filth they lived in, whilst men folk were taken away to do Rome's bidding. No matter the age, they were sent to serve the need of the Empire. Many tribesmen fought bitterly; some gave in. Those that did, had a better chance of survival. Survival was the key to all, to the Romans especially, *for who will do the petty jobs that were beneath us?*

There were many who were collected for imperial gains; the latest batch being members of the Clubrett tribe. They were the most robust of men we ever found... *the cream of Britannia...* as long as they follow *our* way.

We gathered many men for triremes bound for the near east, to a small spit of land which straddled two continents. We captured it centuries ago and our control of it remained a constant challenge to local leaders. A small town on the coast served our purpose... we called it Mentis. There were little minds at work that went mental most of the time, due to the diversified populations. Unfortunately, with much diversity comes clashes a-plenty, especially with those *against* our rule.

A local man called Claudiodufus, who came from the group of monotheists, had served as the Governor of the region. It was an example of those who helped us toward our goal of world domination (*well, the known world, at least!*). As long as they served *Rome*, their rewards would fill their feasting goblets. A *Hail Caesar* was the entry into the good life we had offered. It did not matter where one came from... it mattered to where one goes and that the future was guided under Rome's most spacious wings.

Mentis was not a huge metropolis, but it served as an excellent trading hub. One could buy various items like silks or spices from Africa or Asia. Tall sturdy ships carried cargo as well as people who travelled long distances for business, pleasure or forever-homes.

With the mixed groups came varied forms of worship. We had put up temples to the immortal Caesars, as well as individual gods such as Jupiter, Mars and Diana. Other odd cults developed, as well as hybrids, which amalgamated from these diversified cultures. There was much debate and differences of opinion as to whose god was best and that led to clashes, mostly between fellow Romans and those of the monotheistic tradition. The Monotheists (henceforth called 'Monos') were adamant that their way and God was better than everyone else's...even to the extent to say that anyone of a non-Mono tradition was *wrong*. The problem was, *who was to say?*

We thought of everything to make Roman society a good place to be. However, the Monos were never satisfied with what they had, and wanted more. *Too much, I'd say.* They even went about how this Great Spit of Land actually belonged to *them*! *How preposterous... what a cheek!!* Rome, of course would heartily disagree, unless one became one of *us*.

A splinter group of Monos, calling themselves Christians, began to emerge in the community about this time. They believed in the teachings of Jesus Christ, who lived a few centuries ago. They were ousted by the traditional Monos, who said their way was false and that the fellow they were following was *not* the promised Messiah. We did not care *who* anyone followed in faith, but the Christian's refusal to contribute to sacrificial rites was appalling. *Again, who was to judge?* I certainly did not find it intrusive. It was a quiet, personal faith and very appealing to many people of faith, no matter what their faith was.

Its message preached salvation for all who would repent. *Me, repent? From what?* Hah, I am a soldier of the Roman world and their world was not for me, *yet in secret, I gave consideration.*

Enough of my silly patter and I shall introduce myself. I was born Titus Clunos Coralanus, approximately near the ides of May, about seven and thirty years afore. My surname evolved from a nickname given to an ancestor, which loosely translated to 'Rose Bottom'. I preferred Coralanus, as many of my comrades-in-arms would never let this joke pass. (I still get a-ribbing from them, but only lightly.) I joined the 12th Legion under the great General Silardicus, from the age of eighteen. The good General was someone to be reckoned with, as was proven on many a campaign.

Unfortunately, Silardicus engaged in his most difficult campaign of all... he had fallen in love with a beautiful girl, whose Mono family was prominent in their respective community (*or so they thought*). Before they met, he had secretly converted to the Christian faith and did not make much ado about it. He just got on with his military business... it did not matter *who* he prayed to for success. The girl, who Silardicus fancied (despite the religious differences), he later (secretly) married and eventually impregnated. Her family, the Archevs, adhered to the old faith and gave no regard to *his* belief. Thus, the family was not pleased about the union with the General. They harassed him to convert to the old way and he argued that if he did, he would rather be dead. The girl's mother fumed violently and gave the General an ultimatum.

Of course, as Silardicus was a high-ranking military figure; he could have put the whole family to the sword. *It was a shame he did not*, and in a far-fetched, fleeting moment, he walked away, intending to seek a divorce later on. Pity, the General left the pregnant girl behind with her caustic family. He did return when he heard through various channels that a daughter was born. With a little help from us, he spent time with his new family in secret.

The child was baptised by one of the underground Christian communities, led by the lone preacher, 'Wolf' Harris, before the mother's family had found out. Then, they called the child 'Tia'. I bore witness to this little miracle and began to feel strongly for her and toward the religion Silardicus chose for himself and his little girl. The General, having done right by his daughter, had fled the scene and continued his military service.

This must have been many years ago now, as Silardicus had since fallen in battle against Roman resistance groups. I was present at that skirmish, nearly having the life taken from me. As Silardicus was dying from a spear wound, bleeding out profusely, he spoke to me.

'Take care of little Tia for me. When she comes of age, you have my full blessing if you wish to marry her and tell her I love her, Corr.....'

And then he died.

The burden of responsibility had fallen upon me like a ton of bricks. *Did he mean for me to look after her now?* I looked up, hoping for any further enlightenment, but it was obvious the General meant it for discretion. Unfortunately, I could not do anything about his dear daughter, as the mother's family got swiftly involved and started rearing her in *their* way. So, I would not interfere... *yet.*

The Legion was named after the General ever since, as tribute to the great man. Soon, I was counted for a promotion... but not as a General. That position went to a fellow called Nivien. I was called to the post of Tribune. I had a good friend who stood by me during those years, and acted as my second, the 2-IC, Eos Carmikulus.

I later wondered about that little girl, Tia, and sorely hoped she was cut from the same marble bust as her father was. Over the years, I have seen the young girl with what looked like grandparents; (the ones who opposed the relationship with Silardicus in the first place).

There was no sign of the mother and I wondered what happened to her. Remembering these people were traditional Monos, I feared for poor Tia. It was apparent that her baptism was piss in the wind and taken for nothing. I felt it was ungodly that she would be subject to the torments and prejudices of the older faith. *She would definitely need to prove her salt.*

CHAPTER II

Meanwhile, the Clubrett slaves were arriving at port and being dispersed by auction to those with plenty of money, ready to outdo one another. They were a nameless, faceless bunch, but to someone called Greyrivers (a rich Roman citizen, formerly from the province of Britannia), they were to demonstrate their worth to him.

Greyrivers was once a slave himself, and worked his way up to freedom, and eventually became affluent. He purchased about half-a-dozen slaves to fill his vacant situations. Over time, he lost slaves through illness, death or escape (in very rare instances). Undeterred by the setbacks, Greyrivers would treat his new group fairly and firmly. He had frowned upon slave-beatings, as they did no one any good.

The group were all headed for Greyrivers' villa not too far from town, in the Ansarah Valley (so named in memory of an embalmer, Ansarah, who once lived there). When the embalmer passed away, Greyrivers bought the estate and made it his own, after he earned his freedom, and saved some money.

The new group he bought were put on record as Buckingham, Cateliffe, Nay-Smith, Tudmond, Wilset, and Woodes. Their surnames sounded rather unusual to him, but as he was cut from the same cloth as they, he accepted the oddity. When the slaves were told to change their names to become numbers by the auctioneers (in order to erase their former identity), they protested.

'We will submit to Rome, but under our *own* names, thank you,' Cateliffe stated.

Eos Carmikulus, my second, enquired of such ghastly labels (referring to the surnames).

Buckingham retorted sharply, 'We are Clubretts from Whitfir, in the southern region of Britannia. Our names reflect our trade or where we lived near. Tudmond is short for Tydder's Mound, Nay-Smith works with horses, Cateliffe is short for Cat Lift, Woodes lives in and works with wood and Wilset, well, he's just Wilset!'

Eos bit his lip, waiting with bated breath, asked, 'And what do you do?'

Buckingham laughed, 'I buck the hams!'

My second rolled his eyes impatiently and led the group to a cart, bound for the villa.

On a patrol along the road, I offered my assistance as an escort.

'I never had any use for the soldier,' Greyrivers said, 'But as I need to keep this bunch in line, your effort would be appreciated.'

'Good,' I walked alongside the cart. It went slowly anyway, and I knew it was going to be a long day.

The slaves took notice of me and muttered amongst themselves.

'*Salve*,' I greeted, trying to keep the peace.

Wilset, being extra cheeky, called back, 'Hail, Caesar!'

The group tittered so, but upon them glancing at the sword at my side, they wished they had not.

Cateliffe engaged first. 'So what's a Roman soldier like you doing in a dry-dock of a place like this?'

'I am Tribune Coralanus of the 12th Legion of Silardicus,' I affirmed proudly, 'I volunteered to escort you.'

'What, back to camp?' Buckingham continued his voluminous mirth.

'What do you mean by camp?' *I was hardly amused.*

'We were put in the hold with other prisoners,' Woodes said, 'It seemed like an internment camp to me.'

'We had to put you lot somewhere. This isn't a holiday! You are slaves for Rome,' I insisted.

A pause was held in the air when Woodes asked, 'Who's Silardicus?'

'My former General; now please pipe down,' I ordered.

They settled down a bit, but their plucky inquisitive nature had irked me. I guessed I could not blame them... after all, they were forcibly removed from their normal lives and made to live in this far-off scrap of land which straddled two continents. However, if they were *my* slaves, I would whip them senseless.

'Do you have anything to drink around here? I am so thirsty,' Wilset whinged.

'Some food would be nice too,' added Nay-Smith.

I fumed red-hot in my tunic-under-the-armour. 'And I suppose you would all like a nice hot bath!'

'Ooh, yes… please,' Woodes begged.

I tut-tutted vigorously when Greyrivers assured them. 'We will be home soon and before I put you lot to work, you will get food and drink and have the ability to clean up. Is that alright for you?'

'Thank the gods,' Tudmond exclaimed.

My ears perked with interest. 'You're a Poly?'

Tudmond looked confused. 'A Poly?

Buckingham nodded with understanding, 'A polytheist... a man for many gods.'

'Ah yes, I get it now,' Tudmond acknowledged, 'We are men for many gods. I like the Spirit of the Trees, myself.'

'I like the Water gods,' Cateliffe admitted.

Woodes, whose first name was 'Xan' (as revealed from their muttered chattering), commented, 'I like the Tree Spirits as well, though when I do my work, I feel like I am killing them. On other hand, one can see this action as the freeing of the Spirit itself. So, it could go either way.'

Nay-Smith agreed (poetically), 'It is releasing the trapp'd souls into the sky...'

'...and they fly all around us, o'erseeing our affairs,' Tudmond concluded the sentence.

I could not cross their cultural boundary very well. 'You lot are soddin' weird!'

'To each his own,' Cateliffe remarked, 'So, what does a soldier believe in, then?'

I reflected carefully on that one; thinking, without giving too much away, 'Mars, the god of War and Jupiter, King of all the gods.'

Tudmond piped up, 'You worship a god that condones endless killing?'

'In the name of Rome, yes,' I stated firmly.

The group trembled a bit and I smiled at their reaction. *Seemed I put them in their place!* The path winding toward the villa drew us ever-so-closer to it. The sight was imposing and I have now seen the nerve of it all, an embalmer's estate now owned by an ex-slave-nouveau-riche! I held Greyrivers in contempt for his total audacity of being a show-off. Then I glanced with distain at the scrubby, pick-your-nose-looking slaves and my stomach turned. At least, I must give Greyrivers due credit for having a huge garden to disguise the gross-out smells emitting from this sold-off pack of Britons.

When we reached the villa, huge orchards stood guard on the path where shrubs formed into green sculptures, done by one of Greyrivers' former slaves who had a gift of artistic license. Citrus fruits grew on some of the shrubs, whilst grapes grew heartily in earnest at the rear of the garden.

The house itself had two box-shaped, square buildings on each side, with an rectangular colonnade between them. Built in stone and marble, the place looked like a palace. When it rained in the area, one could hide under the roof, beside the columns, whilst the fruits grew in strength. In bright sunshine, the slaves would pick what seemed like endless bounty and convert the fruits into wine, or other liquors to imbibe, to be later sold on at market. Greyrivers allowed his slaves to have a rationed amount of fruit each day to keep themselves at their working best.

However, some former slaves could not understand the benevolence given to them and, at times, some of the more unscrupulous ones took advantage of the situation.

The new group Greyrivers purchased were hoped to last longer than previous lots. Since all of them were fellow Britons, like Greyrivers himself (long ago), he felt there may be commonality between them to serve a more mutual and beneficial relationship.

CHAPTER III

Another slave came into the fold, not too long after the Britons. He was named Sans-Brys, from the region of Hanlette, in the province of Gaul. Although he was not of the impoverished classes, his reputation at a local academy got the better of my fellow Romans and we duly took interest in him. He was a Professor of Dance, with very unorthodox teaching methods (although he was most satisfying to watch). He demonstrated exotic dancing in between his lectures and, as a result, he was most wanted by the Empire. Again, the Empire did not care who you were or where you were from... if you can serve Rome, then *you* were wanted... no matter how prominent you were in your community.

Sans-Brys was put to work in a public house called *The Knotted Ash*. With loose-fitting and revealing tunics, wearing sequinned sandals, he drew in the crowds and aroused the very best of us. He resembled the angels off the walls of our frescoes, with his oblong face and sandy blonde hair. His eyes were an intense golden brown and his flesh was a pasty white that lent itself to be tanned in the sun.

People were amazed at his moves, sometimes accompanied by a smaller lecture. Though he made use of his mind, we wanted his body. Thus, we came to see his floor show. Eventually, the lecturing ceased, as we were more interested in the dance. Due to the racy nature of his work, only adults were admitted to see him. It was impossible for one not to react, even the older ones. The girls reacted quietly, retreating into themselves and the men just got erections, only to finish themselves off in one of the many private rooms allowed.

Such was the stamina of this new arrival, people came in by the score to see him. He was the main attraction of Mentis and suddenly found himself in demand, mostly to perform, otherwise to titillate. Girls would claw to get at him, with their vicious desires getting the better of them.

The rest thought of it as harmless fun, and found their own gratification as well. I did not mind the setting, as I found it to be a thrill unto itself, and I laughed about it with Eos, off-duty.

* * * * *

I had no one in my life. My career took over much of my time, *married to the army*, as they say. I spent many a patrol watching the little Mono girl, Tia, grow up and I patiently waited... Due to the grandparent's influence, Tia was now known as Zipporah, which meant 'bird' in *their* language. It was either she lived in a gilded cage or she had the smarts to fly away. I so lamented for her, being Silardicus's child, I supported her in my breast and kept her in my prayers. I hoped one day, I could rescue her from that traditional Mono-crap. My thoughts betrayed my sentiments once when I caught her on the main road, with her grandmother. The girl smiled at me and I gave her a wink. The grandmother was irritated by this, and drove her away from my sight. *This became a turning point in my life to seek her....*

After a stint on patrol with my Legion, I walked along one of the back alleys that led to the sea. I was accompanied by my second, Eos, who was willing to stage the scene with me.

A stray cat tinkled by... oh, how I wondered about that! It had a fanciful collar on, with three bells bestow'd upon it. The animal went skittish, and became a streak of mixed-coloured lightning that mine eyes e'er did see.

We reached the path which stood by the sea and I lent on a pillar to take it all in... the blueness of the raging waters, and a sky speckl'd in cloud-dust. I found it breath-taking and pleased that my rank allowed for such frivolity.

A sudden sharp spray had wet my countenance and the inner lining of Eos's uniform had met a further spectrum of dampness. Our armour protected us, but the water had a nasty sobriety about it. It forced one to shake off dilemma, whilst being caught out cold.

The next occurrence revealed a wake-up call that one would rather forget, and one that even our armies could not conquer. A creature of leviathan proportions had awoken from its sea-bed and took its aquatic constitutional. It was a massive whale, with a bluish-white sickly surface from its head to tail-fin. It looked fierce, but so did we, on a clear day. A pair of wizened eyes peered at us, and I had noticed my second had fainted from astonishment. It was up to me to see what this creature's purpose was.

'Hello,' I called out.

A fin flapped in a wave-like motion, splashing all in sight. The resulted water rushed upon the shore once again, soaking more of our uniforms. Eos woke up suddenly, yet upon looking at the whale, he returned into the dead faint. *Some second he made.*

'Greetings,' the whale spoke.

Did I hear correctly?

'I do apologise for my entrance and the mini-tidal wave I created,' it continued.

My mind reeled in disbelief... *a talking whale?*

'I did not mean to give you fright,' the voice went further.

Eos woke again when he saw the whale. He got up bewildered, and freaked out on the spot, his eyes not comprehending what they saw... as for his ears, *well, that was left to the gods.*

I stuttered, 'Y-y-you were apologising?'

'Despite my size, I do claim to be polite. I see your friend hath faltered,' the whale noted.

'Don't worry, he always does that. He's still a good soldier,' I defended, on behalf of Eos.

'So what are two legionnaires doing without their units, eh?'

This fellow was inquisitive for a great beast.

I sat Eos aside. 'Let me deal with this.'

'You do that, Corry,' he put his hand on my shoulder. He went to a pillar and waited.

I faced the whale. 'We just gone off-duty and taking leisure. I was unaware that a creature of your kind could speak.'

'Oh, I get by, here and there. I listen to your many citizens of many nations and colours. I have become fascinated with your society o'er the years, for such is the power of your enlightenment.'

I blushed at the notion that a whale would take interest in Imperial progress.

'However, what I dislike intently, is that there are those wanting to hunt me down. Many fellow sea creatures have become prey to your kind. It disgusts me that they do this in the first place. They come along, to and fro, in their sailing ships, spears at the ready and whoop! Some poor creature cops it. I have learned to evade them with time, but I know one day, I will get it, too.'

There was a short pause, then the whale continued his moan. 'I scream, 'No, No, you cannot have me... I am too big for thee and can pile 'pon y'ship like man on a mattress, sink th'boat and wallop all to death. Yea, I am the great Master of these seas, I am!''

What a conceited git!

'Must be survival, I guess,' I interjected.

'Well, that is Man for you! What are you called Roo-man?'

'I am Tribune Titus Clunos Coralanus. My closest mates call me Corry.'

'And I am Mobiah, from the Attican Seas.'

'Ah, not too far away from us, then.'

'You are far from home,' Mobiah observed.

'We were posted here from Rome. It could have been worse.'

'I always come to these waters on my feeding-rounds. The food is tastier here, plankton or the occasional man, Roo-man or not.'

Now, it was my turn to fright.

'Do not worry, I do not like the taste of soldiers. Your armour leaves a bitter taste in the mouth,' Mobiah reassured with what looked like a smile. (*Could a whale smile?*)

I felt a pang of relief enter my spirit, which told me that this dear creature could make a great ally.... *I had to test this somehow.*

'You stated you've seen things and been around, yes?'

'I have,' the whale answered stoically.

Am I pushing my luck too far here? I was aching to share my interest in the little bird, Tia; the name I shall refer to her as, despite her renaming. I so cursed that Mono family in my heart and prayed sincerely for her and a way to have her... to be at my side, hopefully, as my wife.

My expressed devotion was noticed by Mobiah. 'Your thoughts reveal your true purpose.'

I gazed at him... *how could he know?*

'It's a woman, I bet it's a woman. It is always a woman with you males-of-the-species!'

Damn whale!

'Mobiah, there is a girl and this one is different. She is Tia, the natural daughter of the great General Silardicus,' I admitted.

The whale jumped in his place in recognition of the names. The resulting wave entrapped me within a wall of saturation.

'*The* General Silardicus? My dear sir, not all surnames are filled with glory, but... *Silardicus*!

'Yes, I am enamoured with the little bird.'

'You fell in love with a flying object?' This whale took things *too* literally.

'She is a person, like myself, a subject of Rome, but imprisoned by her adopted family.'

'Do you mean her mother's family, by chance?'

'How did you....,' I then recalled the leviathan's tenacity for observation.

'It was an in-house adoption, I reckon.'

'And she is not happy. I have seen the way she's been treated. Hardly befitting the daughter of a Roman general,' I added.

'Quite, indeed,' Mobiah concurred, 'The Monos have too much power on these shores.'

'We try to override their ambitions, for they strongly believe this is *their* land. Their attitude leads to rebellion, unrest and conflict, which results in the loss of much-needed men. Hence the fate of General Silardicus.'

'Little minds take the big guns down,' Mobiah reflected in a deeply-enriching vocal, 'By the way, why do you call this Tia, 'the little bird'?'

'They renamed her, using a word in their language which means 'bird'.'

'And they are arrogant enough to miss the irony of it. The Monos think they have it all, their God, and their way of life to appease that God. It is as if they stare into a Grand Light, so bright, it blinds one's eyes, as the sun would. Their attitude and exclusivity blinds them, so that when someone comes along to help them see the Light of God, they destroy him. Now, his path is being followed by others, many of whom former Polys, as well as Monos.

'Silardicus believed in this Man, who showed a different way, referred to as Christianity.'

'Yes, the fellow called Jesus. He covered the intensity of this Light, so it would be more tolerable to the human eye. It is ever-present and equally intense.'

Interesting conversation between soldier and whale!

'I still have my gods to believe in,' I said, 'But I do confess a fancy to this new way. I do hope Tia finds it one day; as it is, what they are doing to her is an insult.'

'It would be. You may conquer others, but at least, you leave well enough alone, as long as they serve Rome,' Mobiah stated wisely.

'Amen, brother,' I agreed, smiling at the whale.

It was interesting how Mobiah had described the blinding arrogance and ignorance of the Monos. There may be an opportunity yet, for this to work in our favour.

CHAPTER IV

On a rainy weekend day, the little bird Tia, known within the Mono community as Zipporah, was sitting next to her grandmother at the local temple... a result of enforced attendance. It was all part of the delusional upbringing. The High Priest officiated endless reading of the prayers and scroll text, whilst another fellow chanted in their arcane language (*well, it was not in our Latin!*). These weekly rituals lasted nigh on three hours, far more than one could bear.

Their leader was Shimonn Ben-Oliviyay. He was one who had seen a thing or two in his fifty-something years. His ever-present square face hung like silence upon a wall, seeing to his temple's flock, like a god, but without the omnipotence. He wore a traditional kit consisting of a long flowing robe, a fringed shawl (in which the fringes themselves had meaning), a head covering (bigger than what ordinary folk would wear), among other bits, which he thought would bring him closer to his God.

His attitude was mainstream, bordering on conservative. He felt a grave discomfort toward those who chose to leave the faith and respective community, especially those who sought specifically the word of Jesus Christ. He was deeply saddened by this and although he came from a strict family background himself, he had to learn to keep an open mind to survive changing winds... *and changed minds*. In the recesses of Ben-Oliviyay's mind, it was recalled that someone in his family long ago had, too, sought the word of God through Christ and duly converted. It was never discussed, but made known to him as an example of what *not* to do.

He was curious about these new Teachings and studied them whilst preparing to become the High Priest and subsequent leader of the community. An open mind was kept back then, and now, but it was never taught or revealed to the masses. Any open front would make the more inquisitive tread where they were not really supposed to go.

The little bird, Zipporah, was one such curious creature, and in her heart, very defiant of the Mono faith. There were times when even I saw the look of anger in her eyes as she snuck-spat towards their temple grounds or stuck her tongue out at various 'do-gooders' of their community behind their backs, and especially at the grandmother.

Ben-Oliviyay knew Zipporah Archev was the natural daughter of General Silardicus, the famed Roman soldier. The mother's family, the Archevs, had adopted her, due to the mother passing away. Still, she was being raised in the Mono tradition and that was enough for him. He honestly did not care *how* she was being raised, outside the temple walls. But what annoyed him the most was seeing her continual disinterest in their religion and this disturbed him greatly. *She could be a threat to the community,* if she carried on like this. His main grievance against her was catching her falling asleep during the scroll-readings and the sermons he enjoyed preaching. She would nod-off upon her grandmother's shoulder, perhaps to drift off, maybe daydream. Either way, she was wasting his and her time, and *it was dead obvious she detested attending the service.*

His sermons, however, went on about sticking with the Mono way-of-life and what it stood for. It was exclusionary, claiming the uniqueness of 'not being like everybody else'. At times, they allowed charity toward others... *as long as it was their own.* Ben-Oliviyay harped on moments of the religion's history where the faithful were being tried and tested before God (having dismally failed most of the time). This resulted in an exodus of fellow members leaving the Order. Ben-Oliviyay tried to get his congregation going, as well as collecting the monies they contributed.

So what was it about those outside cultures which made it attractive for Monos to wish to leave their faith? Was it the more relaxed attitude of other groups?

Was it worship in the vernacular tongue instead of the ancient tongue of the Monos? Maybe it was attractive on a social scale where it did not matter what religion one was. Perhaps, it was the diversity of food available which was not consistent with the Monos dietary restrictions. There were many intermarriages where Monos assimilated into the wider society of Rome (as well as into other cultures), and it was thought this would confuse any consequence resulting from these unions. The reality was that people happily blended their cultures into their offspring, often with positive results, and the Monos letting go of their own faith in favour of their spouses'.

Not so with Zipporah, in this case. Her grandmother made certain she would never falter away from being a Mono and Ben-Oliviyay sensed the firm grip on the poor child. He sensed she was unhappy with her circumstance and did not enjoy what the temple had to offer to her. He had witnessed the dire treatment she received from the Archevs, as well as others, especially her peer group. She never smiled much and the older folk showed concerned for her. They always tried to compliment her on her dress sense and attempted politeness. It was good of them to do so, but it did not satiate the real longing Zipporah had. The grandmother always gave influence upon her, including on how she dressed, who she was with, and overall being (*not necessarily well-being*).

The grandmother was a social butterfly and there was much pressure on Zipporah to socialise on such a scale. However, the elder woman's efforts seemed as if she were trying *too* hard. She tried to guide Zipporah in the old way, in order to obliterate any desire toward Roman, or any non-Mono influence. Unfortunately for that grandmother, Zipporah will always be tied to Rome by her bloodline. In casting out the General and preventing any subsequent meet-ups between father and daughter, it was thought that Zipporah would not know any better, and accept nothing else but the Mono way.

Many of Zipporah's peers also caused some difficulty for her, weeding her out as 'different'. She could not fit in, even in the most liveliest youth group meetings she attended. Not knowing her full background, they used to comment about the fact she had *elderly parents*. They were well-heeled in the Mono way, fluent in its language and always discouraged one another from pursuing other faith-cultures. There was also a distinct hatred toward the new way of Christianity.

And so, Zipporah remained trapped in this world of the Monos, always yearning and, more so, suspecting *something* was not right. She had heard of Jesus and the impact He made upon Mono and Roman cultures. There were many who converted away from the Mono tradition and, as her birth-right intended, one day, she would look into treading this path, too. The worst of it remained deep within her psyche which many Monos had affected. She was constantly told that Jesus was not the Messiah and phrases such as 'knock on wood' and 'cross your heart', for example, were never to be used, as they were favoured by the gentile world. *The exclusivity and seclusion was stifling and tormenting to her and it most cruelly had an endless impact on her.*

CHAPTER V

A few days after my encounter with Mobiah, I walked upon the cobbled streets of Mentis, passing by Lobim Lane, where I came upon my sword and heart, my *Tia*. She was unaccompanied, too!

I said to her, 'How now, young lady?'

'Fine,' she answered, 'I've steered my helm through these masked streets of yore; they are so old and crumbly. They smell like ancient bookshelves, don't you think, sir?'

It had been some time since I last went perusing the old Library, but I knew what she meant.

'Oh, how my heart gives way to thee, my little bird-child,' I exclaimed, 'Why go wandering on y'own? '

A dagger surely pressed upon my heart. *Oh, Silardicus, was this what love had wrought upon thee?*

'I'm going on an errand for *them*,' she answered.

'Ah, way past the winding streets of home,' I replied.

'Nah, just to the corner shop to buy some milk for the house.'

My balloon had burst at such an earth-toned revelation.

I purred, 'Can I accompany ye?'

She looked at me, not unkind, yet with baited brow. 'If y'must, but y'must away, 'fore the elders have their day.'

'I shall keep my silence, and self, scarce. I reckon the last thing the Archevs need is a love-sick soldier at th'door.'

'Indeed, and, as it was with my mother, it gave no fair battle.'

'No, my fair child, it did not. But this time, we shall win the battle. Had it not been written in the stars, or even in books, perhaps, for all time?'

'Yea, we shall keep this in confidence, for there is no confidence in passing through their thorny threshold. It cannot be allowed, yet somehow, we must be together,' she surmised.

'I return to the 12th Legion, then, so fare thee well, my princess.'

I leaned in to give a sweet kiss on her lips. It lasted but for a second... *damn.*

Tia exhaled quickly, 'My parting sir; nothing registers in love like a poem.'

'And with a poem, it shall be conquered. With your cooker turned on, it shall be hence. You are a dream and you are my dream.'

'What is your name? You never told me, but apparently *you* know me.'

'Coralanus, but you can call me Corry,' I swooned.

We held hands, firmly, sighing; then, we went our separate ways.

I walked away toward the opening of the main thoroughfare, the *Via Argumentis*, whereupon I glanced toward a doorway on the Lane, and heard a shutter noisily closed. *Were we being watched? Nay, I'll have no spies here... my bird awaited me.*

Along the *Via Argumentis*. a few soldiers had been stationed to keep the peace. Another slave market operated today to bring in a new batch of slaves from outer provinces. I went toward the soldiers.

'Hail Caesar,' I saluted to them.

Eos Carmikulus turned to me. 'Ah, hello there. Good of you to join us at last! We had been worried.'

Yeah, right! 'Nonsense,' I dismissed, waving my hand, 'I was just patrolling an area of the odd lanes. I thought I heard a disturbance.'

My eyes then scanned the street I was just on. I sighed heavily, thinking of my liaison. I must tell someone; *if only I'd known who had slammed their shutters!*

I decided to leave the matter for now, and carried on with my patrols.

Later on, a few of my men took leave for the evening and I spent my time with Eos. We went together to the place where Sans-Brys performed his famed, and possibly notorious, dancing... *The Knotted Ash.*

The air in the venue was aching with anticipation. Soon, the man himself appeared, fully clothed (by Roman standards) and ready to excite his audience. I heard that this was the point when he would give his lecture, with pens at the ready, and his students listening carefully to his fully-formed speech.

As this was no lecture hall, he just cut straight to the dance... and may the gods have mercy on us. He appealed to both men and women alike and both got their fair share of pleasure from the performance. This would be a fine place to bring Tia out on a date. *By Jupiter, I shall have her and Heaven damn the Monos and their stifling ways!*

The dancing began slow to start, and as Sans-Brys did his movements, eyes were wide open to make ready for the feast yet to come (in more ways than one). An outer tunic sped fast in its removal, toward an eager lady (who grabbed it and kept it as a souvenir). The dance soon held a quicker pace, and the accompanying music had caused its drive to become more intense. I caught a glimpse of someone already seeking satisfaction. I grinned at Eos and shown him the fellow, and he quietly grinned at me.

'Looks like he's having a go,' Eos confirmed.

'Lucky, it is allowed here, as frustration leads to mass disorder. We cannot have that,' I dryly commented.

Eos sniggered softly to himself, when another article of clothing was flung away toward the watching masses. *It was a wonder he got through all those clothes...* This dancing was most captivating and my thoughts immediately to the little bird. I thought about our meeting at Lobim Lane, where she claimed she went off to buy some milk. *A likely story*, I mused, lightly dreaming... then soon, *I realised I was getting...*

Sans-Brys had removed another article of clothing, revealing his near-whole self, the important part of which was hidden under a loincloth.

What an Adonis!

The intensity got to my head. I looked at Eos.

'I must speak to you,' I begged.

His face gave a concerned quizzical look, as he turned to face me, or what was left of me, as I spilled myself on the floor.

'Soldiers,' an observer tut-tutted to himself, rather audibly.

'Corry, are you alright,' gasped Eos, as he assisted me off the floor.

'Fine, just fine,' I lied. *No... I was not alright. I desperately wanted Tia!*

Sans-Brys took no notice of my escapade. He was used to that sort of thing, when things got *too* arousing for some onlookers. He accepted this as part of the job and it was *his* job to get it good and proper, despite the human spillages.

The final article of revelation was removed, as was all common-sense in the room. Alas, the movement was over, yet we knew it would not last... *and it was dead certain I wasn't to, either.*

Sans-Brys took his bows to an enthusiastic audience, who applauded wildly, *if* they were able. *At least they kept their business to themselves.*

People drifted toward the drinks area and went to sit on a multitude of comfy elongated sofas. They slowly began intimacy, and personally, I found that I had had enough. The next performance wasn't for another hour and I bore the sudden urge to depart.

I asked my second, 'Could we go somewhere quiet?'

'Sure,' he replied, 'Actually, I know of a small establishment near here called *The Privy Ledge*. It is private-club and soldiers go in free, as a treat from the State.'

Good, phew... now I can release the *other* pressure inside me.

We left *The Knotted Ash* and walked to the gentlemen's club Eos referred to, just down the path from here.

It was hosted by one of the Patrician Senators of Mentis, Benelophan. It was quiet, with real hob-nobs there, whiling away the latter hours of the day.

We found a secluded booth to sit at, away from the rest. 'Twas a soldier's privilege, especially one of upper rank, such as myself. We ordered drinks and a light nibble of my favourite snack, oysters, *which pass'd ye through the gate to get you to where you were going*. They tasted exquisite, and we paid the barman well for the kind service. (Well, we can't have *everything* free, you know!)

However, I had a larger bill to pay.

'Eos,' I sighed.

'Corry?'

'Eos, I've got a confession to make in the strictest confidence, right? I may need your help later; please bear with me.'

'Anything, my friend,' his face looked committed to the conversation.

I slowly got my pride back and told him about my little bird, Tia.

'I'm in love, Eos.'

'Wow... the last soldier who I knew to be in love was the great General Silardicus himself!'

'Yes, and he has passed into immortality and it looks as if I am heading in that direction.'

A silence stood the conversation still.

'Tia is the General's natural daughter,' I revealed.

'The one the Monos call 'Zipporah'?'

'The very same,' I glumly stated... *oooh, I hated that name. She is Tia, first and foremost!*

'Gosh, this is wild news. How are you going to manage?'

'Well, spilling oneself over a friend was a start.'

Eos let out a laugh and I gave him a look which shut down the silliness faster than a slave revolt. Others nearby gave us a glance. Soon, my second composed himself and listened to me.

'I have got to get Tia out of that Monorail she is on. She is headed for oblivion and we must halt this express. This very thing happened to her mother, who suffered to her detriment for the love of our General. I will be damned to Hades if this happens to Tia.'

Eos reflected, 'No, I suppose not. Have you a plan?'

By Jove, I quickly remembered the slammed-shutter incident. 'Not yet, but please send a patrol to Lobim Lane immediately. I fear there may be a spark of issue in the area.'

'Will do,' he agreed, 'What is so special about that alley?'

I bit my lip with sudden anxiety and fear. 'I have a hunch, but if left unchecked, there may be fertile growth which will choke the stalk of my love!'

Eos looked at me with puzzled eyes.

I clarified the allusion. 'We cannot have untamed grass-seed in the midst!'

'Ah... I get it,' he realised with confidence, 'You fear there may be a spy in the works.'

'Worse... if this gets back to Tia's Mono family, there may be more sacrifices than we could handle!'

We shook hands on that note and finished our drinks. We later returned to quarters with the rest of the Legion for the night.

CHAPTER VI

Tia's love for me had loosened a fine line, which did not take much to unravel. She went back home to her grandparents, but tarried on, so as to return at a much later time. She did not go anywhere else, (other than to buy the bit of milk), and walked slowly and carefully, almost as if she were being watched. And watched she was, but by one of my fellow officers, Nivien, who now was privy to my dilemma. He happily joined my ranks to keep control and watch over *the little bird*.

Unfortunately, my earlier hunch was correct in that I suspected something in the area. There was a Mono wench spy, who turned out to be the slammed-shutter Grass of Lobim Lane. I was further informed that she was a local gossip, *keeping a look out for her own kind*. Apparently reported to the grandparents, my meeting with Tia was no longer a secret, and they were incandescent with the news.

Upon returning to the dwelling, Tia was faced with the most heinous row one could never endure.

'Word has it that you were seen with a soldier,' the grandmother interrogated, 'Is this true?'

'I just said hello to him,' Tia (or Zipporah) defended.

A smack was met upon her face, as the grandmother raved. 'Mrs Sellinghah saw you speaking to him, kissing and holding hands. What say ye of it?'

'To keep the peace, I assure you,' Zipporah further defended.

'If you keep this up, you will end up like your mother!'

Zipporah felt sheepish, but was inwardly undeterred. 'So be it,' she muttered.

Another slap hit her cheek as she reeled down upon the floor.

'Do you realise what soldiers do to young girls like you? Huh??' She stared at the girl, with eyes of evil intensity.

Silence paused the rant. Zipporah, by this point, had shut down and gazed off at a distant decorative wall.

Here we go.

'They rape, molest and even kill for their gentile sacrifices,' the grandmother stated, *with ignorance, of course, as she obviously was unaware of true Roman traditions.*

Not a word was uttered from the young girl's lips. She started to cry, crying for that new-found love she sought and found deep in her heart, me... *Coralanus!*

'We do not approve of you mixing with heathen races. We are Monos and that is what we remain. Yourself included,' she carried on.

Never, Zipporah's inner voice protested; shouting out her natural defiance, with heaps of hatred toward the Mono way and this Mono family she, by cruel circumstance, *was forced to live with.*

'We must keep more of an eye on that child,' the grandmother said to her husband.

The husband did not stir from the daily news-scroll he was reading, as if the world around him was more important than the drama unfolding around him.

He then looked up at his wife, 'Zipporah's of age, you know. I cannot see why you must keep her under tabs. It is not like there is anything wrong with the girl!'

'Because she is young and foolish, just like her mother, Susan. She would fall even further.'

'Remember, Susan was ill.'

'What makes you think Zipporah is not?'

'She has a head on her shoulders and I do not understand why you feel the need to shepherd her so much. You are overprotecting her without due cause or necessity. You are stifling her growth. She will be a child for the rest of her life, if you do not properly let go of her and let her be.'

The grandmother was livid by this time and screamed, 'THAT IS NOT OUR WAY!'

The grandfather stood up to the grandmother and gave *her* a smack on the cheek. He then walked out, leaving the two generationally-incompatible women on their own. The grandmother did not falter, and regained her senses, *however twisted they were.*

* * * * * *

A few weeks had passed and it was a day of festivity for the hybrid god, Illumina-Deya. Everyone in Mentis had come to celebrate the good Lady, all except the Monos who *chose* to stay away. I participated in the procession with my fellow soldiers, as Rome's re-planted dignitaries waved at the multitudes. I held myself together, as we soldiers did not wave (and would not under *any* circumstances!).

I perused the endless faces in the crowd, when, lo, have I seen afresh upon myself one who was based in my enemy's camp? *No, no, not Tia!* Wow... but, *how could she be here?* She certainly has made it. Apparently, she was accompanied by... what looked like one of the male members of the family. Couldn't be the father, of course... Silardicus had passed into eternity. She was an only child, thus, this was not a brother... but she was adopted... *could it be an uncle, perhaps?* The man was too young to be the grandfather.

It was odd to see her here, though secretly, I relished the possibilities and praised the gods above. He held my little bird close to him, yet, I wondered how she'd managed to bypass the will of her grandparents to witness this *pagan* ritual in the first place? Of course, I did not care and further reflected that *I* should not smack the gods in the face for such contempt. They had placed the girl I loved right into my proximity, and lo, I would take advantage of this situation to the fullest. *This was too much a delicious opportunity to pass up.* I planned to separate her from the Archevs in order to school her in the proper way (eventually leading to a marital rite to which I aspired).

The procession had concluded and I made my way through the crowd with one thing on my mind. I sought ferociously to find her, so when the time came...

I had requested my second, Eos, to assist me in this undertaking and planned to use him to further my plan later on for the finality. He was only to happy to do so, for we were good friends and he knew of my passion with the little bird. He also knew the story of Silardicus and the consequences therefrom. *We had to get this right.*

I called him over and pointed out my bird and her male *chaperone*.

'He doesn't look too unyielding,' Eos noted.

'See what ruse you can create to get her past him. As there is only one to deal with, you should not have much difficulty. He looks inattentive enough,' I schemed.

'I will oblige thee, my dear Corry,' he assured.

'Well, you must get it done, for there will be a lifelong debt to pay,' I snapped.

Eos had removed his armour, and snuck through the onlookers. It was a most delicate task and he did not want to alarm anyone. I stood by the wall (protecting his armour) and awaited him and *the prize.*

It did not take long for him to reach the goal. So many people were watching the antics of the dancers and erotic performers alike, who entranced all. Eos got even closer to Tia; the chaperone was speaking to her. The chaperone appeared remarkably distracted, as if he were waiting or looking for someone. *Who was he waiting upon?? The grandparents? No... not here... it could not be.* Logic would immediately dismiss such a notion. The Monos would *never* enter a place like this. Eos's curiosity rose to full height and suspicions increased. He further listened and the choppiness of the conversation was too unbearable to ignore.

He boldly went over to them. 'I noticed you were in minor distress. May I be of service?'

The chaperone replied, 'Yes, I was looking for my friends. They were supposed to meet me here, but they seem to have blended in. I am to look after Zipporah.'

'I can see that Zipporah can look after herself,' Eos then turned to the girl, 'Can't you, darling?'

Zipporah smiled at Eos, oblivious to his *true* intention.

'Well, I guess she could,' the chaperone commented, then looked at her in her full-bloomed light, 'Can I trust you to stay here for awhile while I find Simon and Andrea?'

'Yes, Uncle.' She gazed down at her feet. *The signs were present to reveal that all was not well with her.*

Eos thought quickly. 'I can watch over her, if that would give you time to look for your friends and not worry about her.'

The uncle agreed. 'You stay with this gentleman and I will return as soon as I can.'

'Fine,' Zipporah muttered.

He left the little bird to Eos's care. Once the departed had disappeared to look for misplaced companions, Eos signalled to me. *I then swooped in for the kill.*

'Corry,' she exclaimed.

'The one and only,' I affirmed, giving her a kiss. I glanced at Eos, who realised his time was at an end. 'Patrol the area, once you've reaffixed your armour, and see to it that we are not followed by any one or any thing. If that grass is present, dispatch immediately,' I commanded.

'Hail Caesar,' Eos saluted, as he made his way to find the discarded armour.

It was going to be a long afternoon... *but I got my little bird.*

CHAPTER VII

We went around the festival of Illumina-Deya, seeing so many animal sacrifices, endless drinking and carousing in all manners (especially sexual). I went to the snack stall to buy some nibbles Tia and I could share. I recalled the dietary restrictions the Monos adhered to, so I took it carefully.

'You have no issue with food, do you, my dear?'

'No, Corry. I see food and eat it. As long as it does not look back at me,' she replied.

'Good. Have an oyster,' I offered.

She took the item, but could not figure out how to open the mollusc. After I broke the shell in half; she ate the flesh therein. I hastily looked 'round to see if anyone was on the spy... *one never knows with these Monos.* This may have been a pagan festival, but one must constantly be on the lookout. They stick together like glue and (supposedly) hold up one another. In Tia's case, however... no. They could not hold *her* up with a barge pole! *Still, constantly looking back over the shoulder was no way to live.*

I took her around further stalls, when I chanced upon Sans-Brys giving his famous performances. As I did not know him personally, I decided to find his owner, Zahkarris.

'My dear sir,' I spoke up, announcing my presence to him, and introduced myself.

'Ah, a soldier,' Zahkarris responded, startled, 'We do many appearances for Rome, I can assure you.'

'What would it take for a private appearance for myself and this young girl?'

'Oh, that may need negotiation. I must ask though, erm, is she underage?'

'I am but twenty, sir,' Tia piped up. *My little tweeter!*

'Alright, then. Wait a few moments for Sans-Brys to relax from his performance. He had been dancing all day, you know.'

'I understand and we will wait,' I complied and sat on the nearest bench.

Tia whispered, 'What are you doing?'

I stared into her virgin eyes. 'Tia, I am going to help you grow up. You will be getting the Sans-Brys treatment.'

She looked horrified. 'You're planning to take liberty with me, sir?'

'Tut-tut, shhhh,' I comforted her. I tried to calm the poor girl. *Had I practiced indolence upon her?* 'No, I respect you and your innocence. Yet, I know, deep down, you are raging inside and suffering despicable torment at the hands of your grandparents.'

'That is true,' Tia reflected, 'I have no boyfriends, and I do confess a sudden stunt in my progress. They wish me to marry a fellow Mono, to which I refuse. They do keep me under their thumb, like a retarded child, despite my true age.'

Good gosh! The situation was more dire than I predicted. The thought of her marrying another, (and a Mono), chilled my bones and would happily cast me into a pile of war-dead. *No, no, NO! I must quicken the pace.*

'So, you *do* need the Sans-Brys treatment,' I confirmed.

'What is it?'

'He will dance for you and, if you wish, (for this is not mandatory), he may offer you goodly release.'

'A goodly release,' she giggled.

I looked at her firmly. 'Yes, you know. When one gives self-service,' I cleared my throat and pointed to my loins.

Realisation flashed before her. 'I thought you and I were mates in the platonic sense,' she argued.

'We are friends, but it does not hurt to learn from the professionals, and hopefully *further* our friendship,' I soothed.

At that moment, Zahkarris had returned to us. 'He's ready for you now.'

I gulped with anticipation, remembering what happened to me at *The Knotted Ash*. Holding Tia's hand, still looking around, we went inside a makeshift dressing room.

'Welcome, Coralanus,' Sans-Brys greeted. Upon seeing Tia, he smiled, 'And what is your name, dear?'

'Tia, sir,' she answered, 'But my family calls me Zipporah.'

'You're that Mono girl, stuck between two worlds, aren't you?'

Embarrassed at the recognition, she felt downcast and hesitated. 'Ummm, I never heard it put that way before, but... yes.'

Sans-Brys realised a slip-up. I took him aside and explained her situation to him. He nodded with understanding and returned to the young girl.

'This is a small town, so word gets around pretty fast,' he explained, 'The Monos are a very sequestered bunch. They segregate themselves from all, showing an example of prejudice for the children to follow. You see, my parents were Monos, but they were open-minded enough to see other ways, so I was not fully raised within it. My father was musically inclined, and made a scarce living. However, he had plans for me. We later had a disagreement about my future, when my interests turned to the study of dance. He was pleased to see I became a professor, but abhorred the methods I implemented to describe my topic. He thought I was a poof, and disowned me. Mother was sympathetic, but embarrassment did the damage. To this day, I had never reconciled with my family, nor do I heed to the Mono traditions. I changed my name, moved to Gaul, and tried to get on with my life.'

He sighed and I knew not to enquire of his history any further. It was awkward that he revealed himself to us in the first place, and *that* was a revelation we did not come here for. I found it more compelling that Tia's history was no different than that of someone else's... even more so, *the great Sans-Brys!*

We all regained ourselves from the newly-revealed life story to carry on the appointment.

'I am surprised to see you here, Tia,' Sans-Brys said.

'There was an opportunity whereupon I spotted a weak link in the chain,' I proudly stated.

'Well, well. Good for you,' Sans-Brys mused, 'I guess a soldier must see everything on all fronts. Now, let's get started. Do you want a drink or something?'

'A cordial would be lovely.' I accepted his invitation and he gave a glass to me and offered to Tia, who, too, accepted.

'A drink most refreshing,' Sans-Brys cooed, 'A spot of lemon does the trick, no?'

I nodded and the used glasses were set aside. As he had no performances until the evening, I found this opportunity too good to miss. Sans-Brys began his routines for us. I watched, still holding Tia's hand, as the movements became more alluring. He was a beautiful looking man, I do admit, although my interests lay with women entirely. It was more impressive that he danced without the aid of instrumentalists. *Ah, well.* It proved what a professional he was, indeed! *I could now see why he and his father had a row over this.*

Shortly thereafter, Zahkarris stood beside me. 'You know, this may cost you.'

My ears perked up and I realised where this was going. 'Your services are to Rome, and you are lucky you are not dead,' I whispered, staring intensely at him.

The older man had a change of heart. 'My apologies, sir. I will overlook it.' He shrunk back to his tent and allowed the meeting to continue.

I exhaled with relief, knowing my rank came in handy for *any* circumstances.

It wasn't long before the Gaul's routine crossed the border into more sensuous territory, just as a Roman army would do, as a well-spent day's work (but without the sensuality). My mind began to wander again and wonder how my little bird, Tia, felt about all this.

I enquired, 'You alright, dear?'

'Fine,' she said, 'And thank you for taking me from Uncle Marikus. He is such a flippin' bore.'

Ah-ha, so it was an uncle. I was correct in my suspicions.

'You won't get into trouble, I will see to that,' I promised.

'If not, then expect a screaming rant which would last the better part of the night,' she predicted.

'And wake the neighbours, perhaps?'

'Depends how late I return, doesn't it?'

My tone turned dark, '*If* you return.'

She quickly turned to me. 'If??'

'You want to be set free, don't you?'

Tia was caught off-guard. 'But this is so *sudden*.'

'We will discuss that later. Let us carry on watching this,' I remarked and focused on Sans-Brys.

My heart felt amiss to see the doubt in her. I really had hoped she would just go-for-it and want a complete removal. burning the bridges behind her.

The dance now began to make me feel tender in my loins and I put my hand there to check for any pressure.

'May I?' I asked her, indicating at her bit.

'Oooh, that's weird, but since we are friends.' She allowed me to massage her *there*.

It did not take long to feel the wide-eyed screaming release.

She put her hand on mine and massaged me likewise. However, my release was different and it would not look good unaided. At least Tia's clothing compensated for *her* dampness.

'Do you have a cloth or container of some kind?' I asked, desperately, feeling the coming release.

Sans-Brys gave me an old rag. 'Here, have it as a souvenir. Everybody else does.'

The quickening continued, and as I turned the corner, Tia helped clean me up. She licked off the excess from the damp cloth.

'So this is what success smells and tastes like,' she commented, innocently.

By this time, I had fallen over by my body's wrath. 'Yes, my love,' I stood up, 'The sweetened salt of success.'

'Like the oysters we had before?'

'The very same,' I exhaled, giving her a kiss.

By now, Sans-Brys had finished the routine, and ignored our trivialities. 'I seem to have wound you both up. Such is the effect I have upon my audiences and thus my shows are a huge taking.'

'You take me away to another place,' I told him.

'Yea, the bedroom, no doubt, you wily soldier,' he said, 'Still, you both enjoyed it?'

'So that's the Sans-Brys treatment?' Tia questioned.

'Yes, but you had the mild form. There are those who have self-acceptance issues or pre-marital jitters. I know how to set them straight,' Sans-Brys winked.

I grinned and winked at Tia. With our meeting concluded, I shook hands with Sans-Brys and thanked him for such generosity.

'Not at all. I am happy to serve Rome and her children,' he quipped.

I never heard anyone refer to us citizens as *children*, but I shrugged it off.

'Fare thee well,' I said, walking out with Tia.

We departed the tent and headed out toward the crowd. I had not spotted any mishaps, if there were any. My men were on the look-out for trouble. Eos was on guard for that uncle, and to watch for any other Monos which may cause a problem for Tia.

Fears of reports back to the grandparents were high, and it was my responsibility to ensure *nothing* went further than the tent we were in (and surely this festival we attended).

So far, so good.

The evening got underway with participants becoming drunker and lustier than ever. Soon, there were those in kneeling positions, grunting like a raging boar, thrusting endlessly inside one another. It did not matter who it was, as both sexes took part.

And, it was certainly not for children, and my little bird was no child!

I held Tia close and thought of a plan to escape. The activities themselves were escape enough, but her exodus from the Mono's world was imperative.

Soon, Eos found me to report his findings.

'No grasses, and no uncle, either. He did find his friends and they went off together. When you disappeared with Tia, I made an excuse to him, saying she went to a games booth. He then told me to look after Tia and take her home when the time was appropriate.'

That's what he thinks. 'I shall not return the daughter of the great General Silardicus into the hands of wolves,' I vowed.

'No, I do not think the General would approve,' Eos agreed, 'But what do we do? We cannot take her with us to quarters.'

'No, we cannot.' My mind was whirring with vigorous activity. I continued to view the crowds and noticed an oddity. There were slavers in the area, taking away people to put in barges back to Rome.

Screams were heard over the din of the festival and I knew I had to act fast. As Tia was still with me, she was safe, but she could not remain with me.

I soon recalled the British slaves, the Clubretts, who came over some time earlier and worked on the Greyrivers estate in the Ansarah Valley.

'Greyrivers,' I shouted out.

Eos looked puzzled. 'Greyrivers?'

'Remember those British slaves we imported recently? A former British slave-turned-citizen bought the lot and put them to work on his estate. She will be safe there,' I proposed.

'Ah yes… I totally forgotten about that. But what if the Monos come looking for her? 'Tis an inevitability. They will not rest until they find her,' Eos cautioned.

'Eos, duh... there are slavers about.'

'Then we must do right by Rome and General Silardicus,' he concluded.

'Yea, a young maid has been taken away from her father and made to disregard Rome... yet, Rome is in her blood. This is what matters. We must bypass the Monos and head for the Ansarah Valley. Let the Monos *think* she's been taken into slavery. They cannot look for her any further, as slaves normally go abroad.'

'Ah, I see.' Eos got it, but remained doubtful.

'It will work. It must. A young girl's life is at stake. These Monos will cause chaos to our State, and have done so in the past, but I will be forever cursed if they do any nonsense to Tia. The gods will shew us the way forward.'

Eos shrugged his shoulders. 'You and your gods.'

'This is no time for uncertainty, my second. This is a matter of life and death. I intend for us, for Rome, to win. She is of true Roman descent, and certainly not a Mono. Her mannerisms have betrayed that fact to me already.'

Eos realised he had to comply. 'Hail Caesar! For Rome!' He drew his sword and lifted it into the air.

'That's the spirit. Now, spread the word and put the men on full alert. The gods will alight their spirits upon us for the task at hand.'

This was all I could do. Now, I need to get to the Valley with Tia and find Greyrivers.

CHAPTER VIII

After the festival wound down, Tia and I went to the barracks. It was apparent I had to bring her there, as I refused to give her back to her family. Now that the girl was with *me*, I can now see to it that she is looked after well, according to the dying will the General gave me, all those years ago. Meanwhile, I penned a short message to Greyrivers, (informing him of my plans), and had a messenger dispatch it immediately.

We grabbed a bite to eat at the mess and she remained with me for the duration. I then contacted my superior, Nivien, regarding having Tia over for the night.

'It's not customary for one to have a girlfriend with us, but just this once,' he conceded.

'We will be gone by morning. By that time, I shall take horse with her to the Ansarah Valley.'

'Ansarah Valley,' Nivien repeated to himself, 'The embalmer... what do you need an embalmer for?'

'I do not need an embalmer. It is the Greyrivers estate. He took over some time ago,' I said.

'Ah, so he has.' A memory glimmered in the officer's mind. 'Is that where you are taking your girl?'

'Yes, for it is better to place her there, than in the hands of the Monos.'

'Fair deal. She may remain with you... in separate bunks,' he teased.

I gave a very obvious groan.

'Alright then,' he grinned, 'Have her. I will not be responsible for your consequences.'

'I'll be a good boy,' I promised.

'HAH!'

He walked away. Tia and I got cosy in my section. We hugged and kissed and felt very secure in our estates together... *without consequences*.

Tia gave me a glance and smiled. 'I must thank you for your help, though I am wondering about your interest in me. Since when does a Roman soldier give a toss about some silly Mono girl?'

I held her firmly. 'Because, my dear, one: you are the natural daughter of Silardicus, my former General. You may not know this, but his dying wish was for me to look after you, and he made me vow to do so. He also told me to tell you that he loved you.'

'I never knew that, ' she said.

'And secondly, YOU ARE NOT A SODDIN' MONO! Get that in your head. You are a Roman, first and foremost, no matter what your family or that wretched community told you. They lied to you and took your true heritage away, as well as your father, to boot!'

'Gosh,' she sounded exasperated, and showed visible naiveté.

'One day, you will be mine. Your father gave me his blessing, if we should ever marry...,' I dreamed forth.

'Marry?! I did not realise you felt so strongly about me, a flip of a girl, save for your vow to Father,' she exclaimed.

'But, you are *my* flippin' girl and it will not do to forget this. If I die before my time, you will be handed over to my second, Carmikulus. But I do not intend to die! I will slaughter the whole town, if I must, to have you for eternity.'

'Such flattering words, yet by this time, *they* shall come a-looking for me.'

'They will be a-looking and not a-finding. I sent word to my men to spread word that you've been captured by slavers. You recall seeing them at the end of Illumina-Deya's festival?'

Tia thought about it. 'Yes, I do remember now. The slavers seemed very aggressive and many were caught off-guard.'

'And without a guard, *you* could have been one of them,' I pointed out.

'So what is your plan for me, aside from this nuptial wish of yours?'

'Tomorrow, we head for the Ansarah Valley to the home of Greyrivers and a few slaves of his, fresh from Britannia.'

'Britannia? Isn't that far north-west from here? Would I be put to work on this estate?'

'Yes, it is one of Rome's distant provinces. As for working, only if you wish to. You are not a slave as such. We need to get you away from your family, and try to undo the damage and grief they caused you. I trust you are not fond of them, really?'

A silence left a gaping hole in our conversation. I held her closer to me.

I asked again, 'You have no wish to return to them, do you?'

'No, Corry, I do not. I have few possessions, mostly clothes, which I hate wearing. (They were grandmother's choice.) Anything else I had were books on *their* favourite topic. I shan't miss anything.'

'I reckon you would not. Are you ready for this? 'Tis a huge leap toward progress, in a similar manner in the way Jesus Christ eclipsed our eternal gods.'

'Progress is progress; if we must survive.'

'And survive we must,' I smiled at her and gave her a kiss.

'Ummm,' Tia hesitated, 'Ummm...'

'Yes, girl, what is it?'

I noticed a slight fluster about her. *Poor thing.*

'Corry, do you subscribe to those new beliefs?'

'In who? Jesus?' *Now it was my time to squirm. I felt I had been faithful to the gods of yore, yet...* 'I would give the Christ-fellow consideration, yes.'

'So you would turn Christian?'

I sighed, 'Yes, if it is the way forward, but I would still incorporate my own beliefs with it.'

'I see.'

'You?'

'Not sure, but I am dash curious about it.'

'Silardicus had you baptised Christian; as near the end of his time here, he turned to the new faith,' I revealed.

'Wow,' she said, 'So there was much I wasn't told.'

"Fraid so, my dear. Let's get some sleep; we shall have a busy morning.'

* * * * * *

We got up early and I packed a few essentials, mostly canteens, as water is not very plentiful in an arid environment. I thought the ol' girl would do with a change of clothes, so she gladly removed what she had.

'Burn it,' she ordered.

I looked at her in surprise, but the good thing was that she *was* willing to burn bridges. I gave her a red tunic from a stout fellow in tribune class. It was plentiful around her, as she had a slim girth, so I tied it with a belt with extra holes in them.

'There,' I said, 'Now turn around.'

She did.

'You look smashing. Go get washed; we will be eating shortly, then we're off. Meet me at the mess.'

I was most pleased at the result. I did my usual oblations and went off to bade farewell to Nivien.

'I will return, sir,' I stated.

'Good, we need all the men we can get. If it weren't for her sex, I'd recruit Tia. Plucky little thing she is, no? I do know of your vow to Silardicus, but Rome comes first, do remember that.'

'Ah, but if rescuing such a girl is beneficial to Rome,' I argued.

'True. I would move mountains for a girl like Tia,' Nivien admitted, 'Well, good luck to you and yours and may Jupiter's rise fall upon thee.'

We shook hands and I walked toward the mess where Tia awaited me. Eos was there, too, dumbfounded.

'You're leaving us?' He looked concerned.

'Just to get Tia here out of sight of the Monos.'

'Yes, I remember the slavers. I told the men.'

'Good. The Monos do not know where she is and for all *they* know, she could be abroad by now. How imaginative it is to hide things in plain sight.'

'Yea,' he mused pensively, then recovered, 'Can I come along? You cannot go on your own, you know.'

I did not expect Eos would be so keen to help. 'You can join us after we've eaten.'

'Where will you take her?'

'The Ansarah Valley,' I left it at that and went inside to eat.

After having breakfast of bread (with a consistency of a hard biscuit), some meat, honey, fruit, washed down with watered-down wine, I set out for the horses and prepared a litter for Tia on the coming journey.

Eos re-joined me. 'I asked Nivien if I can come with you and he's allowing it. He told me to look after *you*.'

'Mighty kind of him.' I felt chuffed, 'Are you alright in there, love?'

Tia poked her head out of the curtain, 'Yes, sir.'

'Right. Eos, shall we?' I indicated him to mount his horse.

With a covered litter prepared and two horses pulling it, we could not miss. The trek had proved pretty harsh indeed, as we found out a few minutes in. As long as my little bird remained 'caged' with us, she was safe.

Before long, we made it to the outskirts of Mentis, some distance away. I started to feel parched and decided we should rest for a spell. I dismounted and took out the ever-present canteen, taking in a goodly amount. My body began to sweat and I felt damp inside my armour... nearly like the time I met Mobiah... *Tia must meet this fellow!*

I offered the canteen to Eos. 'Drink?'

'By the gods, thank you.' He took the canteen and swallowed a bit more than I would have liked.

He returned it to me, then I went over to Tia.

'You must, my dove, or you will not make it, and I will not have that,' I ordered, giving her the water.

'I wouldn't have refused,' she said, with thankful eyes. She took some and the canteen was far lighter than it was... much to my dismay, but luckily I had brought several with me. *Water was a commodity not to be taken lightly.*

Eos came over to look in on Tia. 'There are two of you, Corry,' she gasped.

I laughed. 'No, this is my second, Eos Carmikulus.'

'How d'ye do? Wow, you look like the twins of the stars,' she stared in amazement.

'A mere coincidence,' I dismissed, 'A hiccup of the gods.'

Eos let out a slight burp. We tittered at the continual mirth.

'So you know of our system, the twins and all that?' Eos stared at her.

'Well, I don't keep my head in the sand, just because others tell me to,' she snapped.

Eos said to me, 'Your girl has got spirit.'

'Yea, to move mountains for... even Nivien would have recruited her for the Legion.'

'Gosh, I wouldn't go that far, but... *women in the army*... nah, that cannot be,' he shrugged.

'It's the General's daughter; remember the vow I took?'

'The great General Silardicus,' Eos recounted with reverence, 'And we have his daughter sitting in a litter affixed to our horses, in the middle of nowhere. Wow. It is so... so...'

'Oh, leave it out,' I pooh-poohed. I then took what was left of that canteen and spilled a little on Eos to pull himself together. His reaction met the mark, as he felt the lukewarm liquid trickling down his head and unto his front.

'Ewh, Corry,' he cried, 'You'll rust my armour!'

'Yes, and you'll rust too, if we don't keep to task.'

'I wasn't trying anything upon your girl, there,' he defended.

'I know. I just needed you to snap out of your reverie. Silardicus is gone, but his spirit is certainly inside this young maid. We must keep it intact.'

Once refreshed, we returned to our mounts and headed for the Valley.

CHAPTER IX

A day or so later, we reached the villa of Greyrivers. The British slaves were still there, working amongst the fruit trees and caring for the grounds. Everyone looked healthy enough, from last I've seen them, and it was apparent that they were treated respectfully. Their labour became obvious, as I gazed on the ripened fruit being picked; their used sheaths had been discarded into a compost pile located at the rear of the garden. The soil beneath the foliage was of dark rich earth, allowing for a plentiful harvest.

I dismounted with Eos and took Tia out of the litter to meet with Greyrivers. We walked past the working slaves, who gave us a quick glance. They then looked quickly at each other, and went about *their* business.

The property was as exquisite inside, as it was outside. *Such show-offs, these newly rich!* A fountain was the centrepiece of the foyer and a grand marble staircase loomed in the background. A few doors led to rooms of varied purpose, including the kitchen, and the more private areas were delegated up those marble stairs. I highly doubted Greyrivers would keep his slaves *here*, but that idea would be extremely rare. Anyway, what did a soldier know and who was he to comment? *I only worked for Rome.*

Greyrivers appeared in a long flowing ivory coloured robe, hanging loosely about his body. His short, straight hair framed a face of benevolent features.

'I thought it was you, Coralanus,' he said, 'I received your message and it sounded urgent. Come in.'

We entered the room he remodelled as a study. The room was originally the Embalmer's work room, where he did the actual embalming.

'I hear you need my help,' Greyrivers continued.

'Rome needs your help,' I declared.

'What would Rome need from me? I dispense enough fruit for the Empire.'

'It is not about fruit; it is about this girl,' Eos remarked.

I brought Tia forward.

'Hello,' my little bird waved nervously.

'It's alright. No need to be nervous,' I prompted, slightly frustrated at her naive nature.

Greyrivers came up to her and smiled, 'And what is your name, pray?'

'Tia,' she announced, 'But my family calls me... '

'Enough,' I impatiently cut her off, and then I turned to her. 'Let me do the talking, yeah?'

She took my meaning and whispered, 'Thank you.'

I ordered her out of the room, whilst I briefed Greyrivers of the situation. She complied at once, like a soldier herself, and left the room. I sent Eos out too, to keep her company. *I needed to do this alone.*

'She is the daughter of General Silardicus, whom I served under, and I swore to him, as he lay dying, that I would take care of her; but alas, her mother's Mono family got in my way. She was being raised in that persuasion by the grandparents, who took over her upbringing after the mother fell ill and died. As you can see, this left her,' I paused, thinking of the correct word, '... wanting.'

'Wanting what?'

I nearly threw in the towel, but had to hang on for Tia's sake. I would admit, I was not the most patient of fellows with my fellow man.

'Let me put it to you this way: she is ill-equipped in dealing with life. She needs to be rehabilitated and re-educated, away from the influence of the Monos. You will be responsible for assisting us in the manner. She will be given refuge here with you and your slaves. I need you to mind her, until the time is appropriate for me to have her. I cannot have her like *this*. And, furthermore, I have my duties. The barracks are no place for a young girl to be.'

'So you will continue to *soldier on*,' Greyrivers joked.

I inhaled passionately and rolled my eyes at the daft comment. 'Yes, and someday, I will marry her. She is not ready and her mannerisms are not fit for a soldier's wife.'

'Those Monos are pretty reclusive and from what you are telling me, her family seems very overprotective of their young charge. What if they come looking for her?'

'We've led them to believe she had been taken by slavers and sent abroad. That way, they cannot look for her. The tide will surely turn against them and I shall have the upper hand, with your help.'

'With my help,' Greyrivers muttered instinctively, and seeing past my nationalistic pride, said, 'Never mind Rome, you want the girl, don't you?'

'This is not an ordinary girl, Greyrivers. She must be treated with the respect she deserves. Heaven knows, her own family did not!'

'I see,' Greyrivers reflected, 'I shall have Tia stay with my wife, Portia-Clare and her servant, Pam Shore. They can help her with the more feminine aspects of living. Bring in the girl and have the slaves brought here as well.'

I left the room and called Tia in. I told Eos to get the slaves inside.

'Corry,' she said, giving me a hug, 'It is very beautiful here. Is this my new home?'

'For the now, yes, my dear... if we can keep your family at bay... and we will,' I promised.

She hugged me more when I saw the slaves piling in. *I could not call them scum now... they were now part of the plan!*

I did a short introduction for them, announcing Tia's presence. They all greeted her favourably.

'So, you are from the province of Britannia? That is so far off,' Tia remarked in awe.

One of the snivelling slaves, Xan Woodes, responded. 'Thousands of miles adrift from a faraway continent.'

She nodded in acknowledgement as Greyrivers gathered them in. With everyone assembled and feeling confident in Greyrivers' capable hands, Eos and I had decided to depart.

'Thank you,' I said, shaking his hand, 'I will come a visit on a weekly basis, if I may.'

'You may do so, sir. I look forward to meeting with you again,' Greyrivers replied.

Tia came up to me. 'I will miss you, Corry. I appreciate all you had done for me.'

'And there is more to come, my love,' I kissed her, 'We must be certain the Monos, and especially your family, do not consider looking for you. We need to keep the peace. Fare thee well.'

My second and I mounted our horses and left for town.

Tia was then individually introduced to everyone, even the slaves (to make them aware of her presence), and assigned to a room set aside for her.

She asked, 'Will I have new clothes, too?'

'Yes, you will. I see that you did not bring a bag with you,' Greyrivers noted.

'Well, it was a hasty and unexpected retreat. Corry had arranged this at the last moment. I had attended a festival with a relative, who then went looking for his friends and shortly afterward, I was met with Corry and his second, Eos.'

'I trust you did not get on well with your family,' Portia-Clare noted.

'No, the soldiers had helped me escape and I had stayed with Corry 'til now,' Tia explained.

Greyrivers had concern for her. 'Is there any reason why your family still has meticulous control over you? I mean, what is your age, ol' girl?'

'Twenty, sir, but they treated me as I were a stupid child, and were stunting progress,' she answered.

'We do not want to stunt any progress here, and we will ensure you will be saved for Coralanus, won't we?' Greyrivers looked at the slaves.

'Yes, Master,' Cateliffe sighed.

'Damn!' Wilset uttered.

Buckingham drew a long breath. 'Do remember all, that we have families back home, yes?'

'We do, or we did, depending on if they are still alive to *remember* us,' Nay-Smith argued.

'Yea, it had been so long.' Xan Woodes looked longingly at Tia.

'Alright, alright, alright,' Greyrivers interrupted the mindless reveries, 'You heard the soldier, we must obey Rome. *This lady is his.*'

'So why can't he marry her now? I see nothing wrong with her,' Xan commented.

'Coralanus needs to deal with her family and other factors, and Tia needs to be re-trained, ready to be a soldier's wife. She needs to calm down from her rough experiences.'

Tudmond found the arrangement awkward. 'It is like dangling cheese in front of a mouse, sir.'

Greyrivers retorted, 'Now, stop grumbling! She will remain with my wife and her servant, who will shield her from the likes of you lot!'

The slaves groaned endlessly.

'ENOUGH! Return to your duties,' Greyrivers commanded.

They filed out, mumbling, 'Yes, Master.' Tia was then left with Greyrivers, Portia-Clare and Pam and spent the rest of the afternoon in long conversation and planning for the future.

The slaves meanwhile went outside to do some digging, planting, picking, and mumbling among themselves, respectively. They stopped talking when Tia and Portia-Clare went out for a stroll in the garden. Pam had held a huge parasol for them, used as a shield from the hot sun and the blazing minds of the slaves.

CHAPTER X

A week or so later, as I vowed to do, I paid a visit to my little bird. She became accustomed to the ease of the household's routines and other tasks Greyrivers set out for her. It had taken some time to get used to the kindnesses bestowed upon her.

I came alone this time, as Eos had done an extra round in my stead. He knew I wanted privacy with Tia and left me to it.

I rode my horse out to find Tia, sitting in the front garden porch, reading a book. She looked settled, passive and, in my eyes, beautiful. Her hair was tied up in an elaborate manner, probably done by the servant girl, Pam. The clothing was most becoming; a fair light blue mix of calm threads woven into the main fabric of summer white. A short necklace of blue marble-effect beads topped the look. I marvelled at the transformation. *The bird was beginning to fly!*

'Tia, my love,' I sang out, dismounting from the horse.

She looked up to reveal a golden honey coloured fringe framing her petite face with brown eyes.

'*Salve*, Corry,' she waved and stood up to receive me.

'By Jove, you sparkle, girl! It is so fetching. Thou'ast captur'd my heart, for sure!'

She laughed and gave me a kiss. 'It is always grand to see you, Coralanus.'

She called me by my full name. *Was she getting formal on me as well?*

'It seems the lessons are proving their worth upon you,' I commented.

'I've been reading about many topics, mostly, from philosophy to the Classics, Latin and religion. If I have any questions, I ask; I was told to expand my mind about things.'

'Well, well,' I said, impressed, 'Are they also teaching you how to be a *woman*?'

She blushed and showed me the book she was reading. It was the Greek play, *Lysistrata*, which had overly feminist tones therein. I smiled back, with understanding.

She asked, 'Will you be here long?'

'A few hours, perhaps. Eos is taking over my rounds, so I have time to be with you.'

'A devoted gesture, I'm sure,' she grinned.

Greyrivers entered the porch where we were sitting.

'Ah, Coralanus, you've arrived,' he greeted me, 'I am sorry I did not welcome you earlier, as there is much to do.'

'Indeed, there is. An estate takes up much time,' I concurred.

'I also wanted to give you and Tia some time alone.'

'Most considerate.' *Now, I blushed.*

'Would you like a drink with me? The fruit has been fair recently and it will prove most refreshing,' he offered.

'Most certainly, I will,' I accepted and looked at Tia, who joined us.

Greyrivers noticed the little bird and mused. 'It has been an interesting week, since we last met. Tia's a willing student and she has taken to her re-training with enthusiasm.'

'That is good to hear.' I took a sip of my drink and turned to Tia, 'We must clear your mind.'

'I know,' she stated, 'And I pray that my earlier hassles will ease off.'

The religious tone piqued my interest. 'Have you decided to explore your faith?'

'I am reading about Roman gods, as well as Christ. I do pray, but I do not do it to anybody in particular at the moment,' she admitted.

I asked, 'So you do not buy into the Mono's interpretation of God?'

'I certainly do not entertain their way of life. It seems the Mono's take on God is similar to Christian interpretation, but it is limited. Christianity is the progression from the old way of thought and brings a new perspective on personal faith.'

'Sounds like you understand more than one could take you for. Spend your time in study and faith will come to you. Heaven will be pleased at whatever you choose,' I encouraged.

'That is a bit of a lenient tone for a Roman soldier,' Greyrivers butted in.

'I give consideration to all. I try to be fair and open-minded to others, except in the case of the Monos. Their exclusivity, arrogance, rebellion against our rule and especially the inappropriate way they treated Silardicus's daughter, is utterly... *diabolical*,' I moaned.

'You did what you could to get her freed of it,' Greyrivers said, 'I am surprised you asked me to help you.'

'It is either you help or rejoin slavery,' I asserted. *I gave him no option.*

'Wait a minute, I am a free citizen,' he argued.

'Yes, you are, as long as you continue to serve Rome, in *any* capacity, or whatever the need.' *I, of course, had a greater need.*

He nodded, 'So be it, Coralanus.'

'You can see what is at stake here, good sir; my honour to the General, along with this girl's life.'

We gazed at Tia and agreed she could do better and enjoy a more fulfilling life, than a life being stifled by her family.

'You are in good hands,' Greyrivers assured, 'When your visit with Coralanus is concluded, please report to Portia-Clare for your next task.'

'Yes, sir. Thank you.' Tia came over to me and Greyrivers returned to his work.

We resumed our walk and chat outside within the perennial gardens and fruit trees around us. We were stared at by the working slaves; some were doing gardening, the others went off picking (*picking what, I durst not think*). Despite the bustling labour, many eyes focused on us. Tia waved to them.

I found her response to them unusual. Knowing she had never been exposed to slavery before, I felt I had to explain.

'They are slaves, Tia.'

'So what? They are human beings at work. It is good to say hello. They deserve that much. Just because others leave the dirty jobs to slaves does not make them less a person, and to be treated like shit,' she argued.

'Are you defending the slaves, my girl? You're getting philosophical.'

'Why should someone be put down due to the work he does?'

I stopped and took her to a quiet alcove, out of earshot of the slaves. 'It is more than that, Tia. These people are the lower rung in society. They have no rights.'

'I did not have rights,' she glared.

'You were a child, then, love. Your family obviously did not give you much privilege.'

'No, they did not. The worst part was that they judged others, especially me. Who is to judge anyone?'

I could not find an answer, and I sensed this conversation needed to veer away from her family... *fast*. I had to think of words to comfort the little bird, though I did not want them to feel lightly said.

'No one. You know, with the knowledge you are gaining and your gracious attitude towards others, I think you would make a good Christian. That may be your answer. As the faith is no longer outlawed, I suggest you pursue it.'

'What about you, Corry?'

'I will reconcile my faith in my own time. I am more concerned for you. You need saving. I am a soldier, and need no trivialities at this time.'

'Could Greyrivers instruct me on this matter?'

I contemplated quickly and remembered the outcast hermit who baptised her, 'Wolf' Harris. As I was present at the event, I felt it would be a good measure she meet Master Harris.

'I know someone who is an expert on the subject. He lives in the desert, and had baptised you as a baby. I was there as a witness,' I revealed.

Tia's eyes widened. 'So you can *prove* I was not a Mono to begin with, despite what lies that family spread about me?'

'I can, but I will not confront your grandmother. It might, shall we say, get a bit messy. I do not wish to expose you to such savagery.'

'Putting evil to death, I would hardly call savagery,' she flippantly said.

Did I hear that correctly? Had my little bird grown more than just wings?!!

I composed myself. 'I have an idea. We will discuss it with Greyrivers. Come, love.'

We went inside the villa and I headed straight to the study. Tia stayed in the atrium.

I called out, 'Greyrivers?'

He sat up, 'What do you want, Coralanus?'

I came into the room and sat across from him. 'I wish Tia to meet Master Harris.'

Greyrivers stood up in recognition, 'The lone Wolf? The known beggar?'

'He is more than that. He is a self-confessed authority on the Christian faith and Tia wishes to pursue it. I bore witness to her baptism, which he performed for her when she was a baby.'

'Oh, I see. Sounds like her life will take a turn, then. If that is where she is going, then I must allow it, for her sake.'

I got even greedier. 'Would you be able to accommodate him on your estate? Your place seems big enough.'

He mulled it over. 'Get Tia in here, please.'

I walked out and retrieved my little bird. We sat before Greyrivers.

'Tia,' Greyrivers asked, 'Would you be willing to meet a dear fellow, that Coralanus here knows, who lives rough out in the desert?'

She answered back, 'Would I live with him, too?'

'Do you like rough living?'

'Ummm,' she hesitated.

I stepped in. 'Pardon the meaning, my dear. It is like the barracks, but far less civilised.'

'Oooh.' She made a face.

Greyrivers resolved, 'I will put him up, if I must. The desert is not fit for a young girl like you, even if a great man lives in one.'

'I can go out there and arrange it,' I offered.

'Splendid,' he chimed, 'We will clean him up a bit, too, and turn him into a real professor.'

Tia giggled, and I snorted, 'He probably is one, under all the dirt.'

I heartily thanked Greyrivers and parted company.

Tia followed me out. I held her close to me and gave her a kiss. 'I will return with the fellow, my love. This man could help you greatly. I do not know him well, but I do remember him from my younger days with your father.'

She bared emotion with a romantic gleam. 'I would have loved to see you from long ago. I bet you were even more hotter than y'are now.'

I winked at her, 'Age can make one becoming. It is all interpretive, my dear.'

'I did not think you would care so much to get me out of *my* desert to teach me.'

'We shall move a mountain,' I paraphrased Nivien's earlier words, 'If it helps you better yourself; but a girl like you in the Master's harsh territory, nah. You deserve better, so we will bring him here.'

'He sounds very dedicated to his belief.'

'He is and if it were up to him, there would have been a church in Mentis. Long ago, the authorities of that time had not acknowledged the Christian faith, and, as Rome did, had persecuted Christians. They even threatened 'Wolf' Harris, but he was clever enough to live out the gospel in the wilderness, to see how it *really* ticked.'

'A complete John-the-Baptist wilderness lifestyle... phew, I cannot understand how he does it,' she muttered.

I went closer to her and gently touched her nose with my finger. 'Ah, you're learning. Although he chose to be isolated, there are those who go to him for baptism and instruction. They give him food and drink in exchange. It's a complete display of Christian teaching in action. He does not threaten our rule, and we leave him alone. Those whom he converts, we keep watch over, but they carry on what they've learned from him and keep to themselves doing so. In the past, some of us caught fire over it, like your father did, but we kept it to ourselves, as it would not look good for a Roman soldier. It is merely a personal matter and we leave it at that.'

Tia just stared at me... in total astonishment. She then smiled and felt proud to be branching away from her spiritually impoverished upbringing. She was ready to renew her life and I *so* wanted to be a part of it.

We embraced, then I walked off to mount my horse and left the property to find the lone 'Wolf'.

CHAPTER XI

The landscape of the desert terrain was harsh, indeed, all-round. There were rocks, small and large, caverns where one could set up a hovel, and a sun that glared daggers at all who were under its gaze. A river lay a mile or so away, so it was necessary to have a daily ration in the early morning and evening to survive.

This was where 'Wolf' Harris lived. Originally from Britannia, he was captured young to become a slave, and shipped off to Mentis, many moons ago. He worked out in the fields, like many did before him and after him, for long hours. It was tolerated for a time, yet, when things got rough, 'Wolf' Harris got rather irritated at his situation. *It was clear that his gods were not helping him.* There were those around him who preached the new faith of Christianity, which he had heard about and made inquiries.

Once he learned more about this faith, it was soon apparent that he wanted to be part of the action and help it grow. The Roman leaders of his time, as well as the Monos, found the new religion abhorrent and decided to put an end to it. This did not deter him and one day, he had fled the fields and wandered for many days to seek his true calling. Amid many sun-exposing hallucinations 'Wolf' Harris believed to be visions, he was led to safety among the caves in the Ansarah Valley. Many citizens, who wanted to follow Christianity, quietly sought him, in secret, where he instructed them and later baptised them in the nearby river. *They left him better people for it.*

'Wolf' Harris's first name was unknown. Everyone equated him to a lone wolf, so he was referred to as such. He did miss his early years, back in Britannia, where the gods ruled and people accepted life as he knew it. However, Rome was in charge and infiltrated all levels of British society of the time, including the spiritual. They fused their gods with the local gods to create spiritual hybrids that everyone could relate to.

Master Harris knew a river near his home that he used to call 'Syd', for some reason or t'other. He did not know why; *was it a god or just a reference point?* He did not know and thought nought of it. He carried on his little tradition and called the river in the Valley, 'Syd', too (but *this* time, he did not think of it as a god).

People from town, who sought his help, had brought with them various writings of the new faith and he read them with zeal. He had his own interpretations, naturally, which he shared with his visitors. As the Church was not yet formed, the fluidity and imaginative views of the belief needed to be refined into proper cohesion. Too many people put their viewpoints in, and it could get very muddled at times. It had a long way to go, now that one could explore it more; as it was recently becoming part of Roman culture, one could happily do so.

* * * * * *

As the heat became more acute, upon entering the outer territory of the Ansarah Valley, I needed to take a rest. I dismounted, had a quick swig from my canteen and took a good look around. The area was a fair sight, but unfair to anyone who would want to live here, exposed, for whatever the purpose.

I walked my horse to what looked like a cave entrance. I peered inside, hoping it was not a wild animal that lived there. I paused and waited quietly; the sweat had run a marathon on my back and I had sorely wished I took the liberty of removing my armour, at least, back at the Greyrivers residence. Since there was nowhere to put the damn thing, even if it was removed, I certainly would not leave it here. So, I stuck it out, with faith, that my ever-resounding silence will see me through (*and find out who in Hades lived here*).

Suddenly, I heard rustling, and my hand went instinctively to my sword. Then, there was a sound; it might have been human, for it did not resonate with growling. I saw a few plants about the place, gasping for water. I took my canteen and sporadically spread its contents on them. *Maybe that new faith had rubbed upon me.*

The wait was over as someone emerged from the cave. He was a tall man, amply built, and had a kindly mature face (like a cured cheese), with eyes showing bags of character. He was weathered a bit, as one would be when one lives 'out there'. I recognised him straight away... it was 'Wolf' Harris, albeit many years later. I noted that he continued his simple lifestyle of prayer and devotion from last I saw of him.

'Hello, there,' he said, noticing the wet patches on the fauna, 'I see you've been watering my plants. Thank you.'

'Not a problem.'

'What brings you here? Instruction, indoctrination?'

'I am Tribune Coralanus and seek your help,' I answered.

'Coralanus, eh? You used to serve Silardicus, didn't you? I remember baptising his daughter; I have baptised so many now, but a General's daughter is one I could never forget. Have you seen her recently and how is the little darling?'

'She is fine and living nearby at the Greyrivers estate.'

'Greyrivers took her in?'

I sighed, downcast at having to inform the good man what had happened to my little bird.

'She was taken in and raised as a Mono by her mother's family. I was supposed to look after her when Silardicus died.'

'Oh, Silardicus died? Too bad,' he shook his head, 'So, how can I help?'

'She is expressing an interest in the Christian way and feels her Mono background is hampering her objective.'

'So, you've come to me, eh,' 'Wolf' Harris smiled.

'You will be put up at the villa, in exchange for your teaching.'

'Why would a Roman soldier have such a vested interest in... what was her name again?'

'Tia,' I stated.

'Ah, yes, Tia...,' he trailed off in a trance.

'Silardicus asked me to take care of her and I vowed to do so, but, the mother's family...'

'...got in the way,' he finished my sentence.

I nodded, 'Mmmm. I got her away from their burden upon her, and she is recovering at the villa. She needs to get past her issues, before moving on to new pastures.'

'I understand. A new life with old problems can be unbearable indeed. That is what Christ had preached about when he used old wineskin imagery to create a parable around the concept. He talked about forgiveness and loving thy neighbour, in addition, to exemplify the new life. However, I see in *this* case, it may prove a bit challenging.'

'Ah yes, Christ never lived with Tia's grandmother. I am sure Your Lord will allow for some *invention*,' I said, smugly.

'Perhaps. Are you conscripted to the faith?'

'No... well, not officially. I have my gods, but see no reason not to believe in yours.'

'Well, well,' 'Wolf' Harris whispered audibly.

'I watched Tia from a distance as she was growing up, and found she had been treated disgracefully by her grandparents, who took over the raising. It was at the recent Illumina-Deya festival when I had her sent away. I saw slavers rounding up for the Empire and took the chance in making her family think she was taken by them. Of course, I sent her to Greyrivers and now I seek you to finish the job of rehabilitation.'

'So, it's up to me, then,' he acknowledged with a smile.

'I would not put you as the final hinge, but you will contribute greatly to Tia's learning and well-needed life skills.'

The older man looked at me with slight suspicion. 'You love her, don't you?'

I broke out into a grin that could not restrain itself. 'I do admit, yes, I am deeply in love with her. The General gave me his blessing and I shall take that offer very seriously.'

'I think you are very bold in taking Tia's matters into your own hands.'

'It was a necessity for Rome,' I defended.

'More like a necessity for yourself,' he pointed at my lower region, 'I know what soldiers are like, and soldiers with vows to keep to Generals and their children, could prove... most unyielding.'

'I shall not yield to disarmament,' I felt my voice rising slightly, 'I shall have my little bird, if it takes all of Rome to keep her!'

'I note you've given her a pet name; very amusing... but, what about her, hmmm? Does she feel as strongly for you, as you do for her?'

'I believe I can make that bird fly and she will love the new wings I give her.'

'Be sure you give her solidarity first. It sounds like she needs good care.'

'Her newly formed bearing has rendered fruit to be shared by all,' I resonated loudly.

'Wolf' Harris looked aghast, 'Wha-- ? Is she pregnant already?'

'No, I would never do such a thing,' I retorted, then admitted, 'Alright, we cuddled and kissed. There is too much to do *with* her than *to* her at the moment. The old ways had taken their toll.'

'So they have... let me collect a few things. I'll be just a moment.'

'Thank you. They are waiting for us,' I said, leaving him to it.

He did not have much to bring; being a hermit, one does not acquire much. He had a few scrolls about and he put on his best from the wardrobe. He was willing to leave his old life behind... *for awhile*.

CHAPTER XII

On the road toward the villa, 'Wolf' Harris and I shared the horse between us, each riding in the saddle for a spell and alternating. It took the better part of the hour to get there and we did not pass much, as this was a lonely and desolate place. Conversation was at a minimum, in order to conserve our energy.

Overall uneventful, the journey was as lonely as the passage travelled, and my thoughts were constantly on my little bird, Tia. I had wondered if she would get on with Master Harris and whether or not she would take on the new faith by her own choice. I wholeheartedly knew all too well that her family pushed her into *their* way and she, in due credit, had resisted them... she merely *went along with it*. I would happily convert to the new faith, too, but best not voice the opinion... for now. *No one cared about the opinion of the soldier anyway; usually, he did not live long enough to make one.* What I felt was important for the moment, was *her* interest in it. That was more than satisfactory.

A passing bird had flown by, heading for the coast. I remembered my atypical friend, Mobiah, and wondered how he was doing. It had been some time since my last visit and I recalled fondly that it was most enlightening. I thought about seeing him again, this time, with Tia. I believed she would love the novelty of a talking, highly justified and righteous whale.

We soon reached the outer path of the villa with 'Wolf' Harris in the saddle. I led on by sandaled foot, and realised my feet could do with a rinse-off. As we made our way, I saw the many slaves that were working on the garden. Master Harris looked keen, as if he saw a congregation in the making. However, I was unsure if that was possible. A multitude of eyes looked up at us, inattentive to their tasks, staring at the gentle man in the saddle. I noticed they were muttering to one another, with curiosity stimulating their minds.

Someone, who I never seen before, had noticed the slave's lagging and verbally whipped them into shape.

'Keep on, lads. This isn't a parade,' he shouted at them.

Ah, another of Britannia's natives... must be the accent.

We stopped finally at a hitching post where I tied the reins and 'Wolf' Harris dismounted.

'Thanks for the ride,' he panted, 'I could've died out there. Do you have any water upon you?'

'Yes,' I gave him my canteen, 'I will take you to Greyrivers and he can get you settled in.'

He smiled at me, drank a bit, and returned the canteen. I led him into the house.

Master Harris was amazed, as he looked around the building. 'Wow, this is grand, isn't it? So, I will be living here?!'

'It was agreed; you are to remain here to instruct the young girl,' I replied, dryly.

'Young girl? Ah, yes, Tia,' he remembered. *Being old clearly wasn't what it was worth!*

'She is eager to meet you,' I said, 'And has questions regarding your time in the wilderness.'

'And I'd be glad to learn of *her* wilderness experience,' he chuffed.

'Takes one to know one,' I thought aloud.

Greyrivers heard our voices in the atrium and approached us.

'You must be Master Harris. Welcome to my home.'

'And what a home it is, sir,' he replied, 'I saw your workers in the garden as we passed.'

'Yes. Slaves to you and me,' Greyrivers intoned.

'No man is a slave in the eyes of God,' 'Wolf' Harris stated.

'Ah, that is a matter of opinion.' I began to sense debate, which I needn't get into. 'I will be getting off to base.'

'God's love is not beyond the soldier, you know. Remember the centurion at the crucifixion.'

I did recall that a bit... the ol' fellow believed, when Grace stared straight at him.

I smiled back. 'I do appreciate your concern for me, but alas, my destiny lies elsewhere. Please take care of my girl.'

I left the company and rode into town where we were stationed.

'Rather tetchy, isn't he?' 'Wolf' Harris commented.

Greyrivers noticed it, but was dismissive about it. 'He's just a soldier, but he's got this debt weighing heavily upon him, with regards to this girl. You have been removed from the caves of the beyond to tend to her instruction.' He then called out to the servant, 'Clarence?'

A tall fellow, slightly bald with greying hair came into the room, and spoke. 'Yes?'

'See to Master Harris's quarters and fetch Tia in for me, will you?'

'Will do, sir,' the servant walked off with 'Wolf' Harris.

Greyrivers gazed outside, staring at the workers. He wondered if they could do with Master Harris's instruction. He sighed, knowing the huge takeover the new faith had on Rome. He had contemplated the possibility... *if it was good for the Emperor, it was good for him.* He left it at that.

Outside, the slaves tittered even more. Restless jumpiness entered them, when they saw the newcomer arrive on the estate.

Xan Woodes guessed, 'He must be a teacher of some kind, but there is something about him that seems extraordinary.'

Buckingham had a good idea. 'I think that is the fabled 'Wolf' Harris, who lives in the desert and preaches a new form of religion.'

Tudmond looked worried. 'Do you think he'll preach it to us?'

Buckingham answered doubtfully. 'I think he is to instruct that soldier's girlfriend.'

Wilset sighed, 'We could use a little teaching around here, for a break. My back is sore.'

Nay-Smith, unfettered by the manual labouring he'd done, was impatient with the whinging. 'Pipe down, and get on with it, before we get told-off again!'

'They couldn't hurt us. Greyrivers had been most generous,' Xan defended.

Tudmond asked Xan, 'Why do they call you Xan, anyway?'

He replied heartily, 'My mother was quite taken with Alexander the Great and she named me for him. Though as a pet name, she chose to differ from the traditional Alex or Alec, so I am henceforth known as Xan.'

'You ain't great... you're a slob like the rest of us,' Tudmond growled.

'Now now,' Buckingham interjected, 'It is not a matter of who is great or who isn't. The point is that we must work together, or be punished, probably separately. Yeah?'

'Well, what in Hades makes Xan so special?' Tudmond rang out with jealousy in his voice.

'My mummy loves me,' Xan cooed.

Tudmond took a chunk of dirt and threw it at Xan, who ducked and the dirt showered against the stone wall next to him.

'Nyahhh, missed,' he teased.

'Get out of it,' Buckingham scoffed.

'I never knew my mother,' Nay-Smith reminisced.

'I never knew my father, yet I bear his name,' Wilset griped.

There was silence and an odd 'Awh, shut up' shouted from a distance.

Tudmond reflected, 'That soldier's girl... she's a Mono, isn't she?'

'She is, but their way is anathema to her, so I've heard,' Xan said.

Tudmond was aghast. 'What the f--, where did you learn such big words?'

Cateliffe finally spoke, 'A few of us are quite educated. It isn't our fault that we were called to be slaves for the Romans.'

'Spoilt shit,' Tudmond muttered.

'That girl is here to be groomed for the soldier,' Buckingham remarked.

Wilset moaned, 'Why can't *we* have her?' *It was obvious the truth had not registered with him.*

Nay-Smith glared at him. 'We are slaves and even shit is too good for us.'

'Nonsense! I am certain we could have more, if we tried,' Xan thought optimistically.

'We are damn lucky we got what we have already. Why push the boat? You'll only get in a bind with society.' Buckingham's view resigned to the oblivious nature he was put in.

Nay-Smith sounded more hopeful. 'Not many of our type have such gracious masters like Greyrivers.'

The slaves grunted in recognition and carried on working, with some still grumbling like a minor earthquake.

Meanwhile, 'Wolf' Harris settled in and waiting in the study, ready for the off. Tia was made to look her best and went in for her meeting with him. Greyrivers asked Clarence to get some refreshments and keep an eye on the slaves.

He addressed Tia and 'Wolf' Harris. 'Make yourselves comfortable. I will be brief, for there is much to do. I was told you, Master Harris, are the best source of this new religion...erm, Christianity. Tia here is interested in pursuing this new faith and you came recommended...'

'I am most flattered,' 'Wolf' Harris blushed.

Greyrivers finished his sentence. '...recommended by the soldier, Coralanus.'

'Yes, I have met him. He took me here, too, which I found most charitable of him.'

'I agree, charity begins at home. However, it is the soldier's wish that you help this young girl.'

'I will do my best, sir. I was wondering if your workers would be interested in my instruction as well. Perhaps yourself?'

Greyrivers smiled, thinking of the offer. 'I will consider it, but one thing at a time. Tia is your priority. The slaves can be taught later, if need be. This seems the way forward. The old order is losing its grip, shall we say.'

Master Harris agreed, 'Indeed it is. Rome is evolving into something other than itself, possibly devolving. Either way, I will do as you ask.' He gave Tia a smile, 'It will be my pleasure to instruct you, as your father would have liked.'

Tia was surprised. 'You knew my father?' She then calmed down, rationalising her way through the conversation. 'I think it would be fascinating to examine the faiths, old and new; you know, to sort of compare notes.'

'I can tell you this... they cannot compare. One is steeped in the past and unyielding toward change. If it does change, in any way, it loses its cohesion and becomes something *other* than what it was intended to be. The newer faith emphasises the relation toward man and God and man with each other, mostly the latter. If we cannot get on, then how could we worship God with a whole heart?'

Tia reflected in silence and drew a long breath. 'Long haul journey, then?'

'When you are ready, we will begin,' he said.

Everyone left the room to commence the enlightening ahead.

CHAPTER XIII

I rode into our town barracks when Eos came up to me, worried.

'You need to report to Nivien, Corry. He's not too pleased at your prolonged absence.'

I dismissed it with a wave of confidence. 'I shall be alright. It was for a good cause.'

'What happened out there?'

'Let me explain later. If Nivien is as anxious about me, as you say, I had better go to him,' I exited the area to find my superior.

I walked away from him and entered a small room where Nivien stood before me; *it felt like I was being drummed up for a court martial.* His face looked like a scarlet of horror and he pulled no punches about it.

'How long did you say you would be away from your duties?'

I sweated, hoping I could get myself out of it. 'As long as it took to settle Tia and Master Harris, sir!'

'That is not good enough, Tribune Coralanus. You took too much liberty, leaving poor Carmikulus to do the nasty bits in your stead. You are to be confined here until further notice, unless you are on your scheduled rounds.'

My eyes watered. *Did he say confined?*

He went on. 'You will not have any unscheduled leave, either, for any reason. Do you understand me?'

'Yes, sir,' I saluted.

'A servant from the villa in the Valley had come by to leave you a message. I put it on your bed. Now, dismissed,' he shouted the last bit.

I went back to my bunk and found the message waiting for me. It was from Tia. It read:

Dearest Corry:
I am doing fine, under the tutelage of 'Wolf" Harris, whom you recommended. Greyrivers has been most kind to me. I do help out on occasion in the house, so I do not feel left out. I am awaiting your return, and hope we can pursue life together soon. With love, Tia, Your little bird

I sighed as I rolled the message and put it into a small folio in my dresser. I laid out on my bed, thinking of her, as well as recent times. Yes, I had been naughty by getting *too* involved, but with the promise of the girl and my desperately wanting her, it was truly unbearable, to say the least.

It seemed she fell for me, as I for her. She was a pretty soul, when I turned up that day, all in her finery. She did not seem to be the caged person I once knew. I was happy to help her, and in my arrogance, I charged toward her like a raging bull. This did not deter her from loving me and the attention was most welcomed by her. At last, I've gotten her away from that mess of a life she was pushed into, and gave her a more reasonable alternative. I prayed the story regarding her being taken by the slavers would continue to prevent her family and that community from searching for her. She was getting on well in life without *them*.

And a life without that family was worth all the court martials in the world!

I began to nod off, in a dozy, bored state for a short while, when Eos had interrupted my dream.

'Corry, Corry,' he shouted, forcing me awake, 'Tell me what happened!'

I gave my head a bit of a shake, when I came to. A sigh left my lips. 'I was grounded.'

Just like my little bird in the past. I realised my position and hers (beforehand) were similar. I was duly ashamed of myself and thoroughly embarrassed about it. I was not really in the mood for a chat, but I daren't dismiss my second. He was too good to me and he might be needed later for the grander plan.

'Yes, yes, I know about that,' he snorted, 'What about Tia? How is she, and all that?'

'She is thriving in the Valley. Broke out of the shell nicely and looked stunning, last I saw her. I helped 'Wolf' Harris, too, out of the desert and into the Greyrivers villa. I recommended him to instruct Tia on the new faith and I left her in good hands. My time with Master Harris was what delayed my return.'

'Nice to hear your bird is doing well. Anyway, the lads are going out. Do you want anything?'

I grimaced... *I wanted everything and the world.* 'Could you bring back Tia?'

'Sorry, we're not going that way, Corry,' Eos lamented.

I deeply sighed again. 'You lot get on, then. I will be fine.'

'You do not *look* fine.' *What a friend!*

'I am,' I insisted, 'Go have yourselves some fun. What are you planning?'

Eos stared at me. '*Knotted Ash*, anyone?'

'Ye bastard,' I shouted, throwing a small cushion at him. 'Send Sans-Brys my regards and let him know Tia's doing alright.'

'If I see him, I will discreetly pass the message.'

'And also check to be certain there is no Mono activity regarding Tia.'

'Will do. See you later,' he saluted to me and left.

Where was my heart now? I could not go out with my friends and fellow soldiers, especially to *The Knotted Ash*, where I first saw Sans-Brys. I could not visit my darling Tia, nor watch out for those Mono spies, waiting to tell-all to her grandparents. *Something had to be done and done with.*

I meandered further in my mind, thinking about her still and my duty to Rome, as well as my vow to the immortal Silardicus. The comments regarding my involvement with Tia as a personal matter, rather than a Roman one, cut deep within me. I honestly thought I was serving Rome by removing a young girl from our enemy. I thought I was helping my General by looking after her; alright, a bit late in the game. But still, I was passionate in my state of being and being with *her*; she meant the world to me. *Was it an obsession?* Anyone can be blinded by anything and from everything, *but for me, it was too late...*

I then came to the realisation that I wanted Tia more and wanted out of the Army. *But how?* The only way a soldier left the Army was to be killed in battle or via a buy-out, which was beyond my means.

But this was a more glorious battle that has ever been fought, for all to see. My decision, though, as rash as it may seem, will be considered for a later time... IF I survive.

I carried on dwindling along in my mind 'til I fell asleep. I hoped a ready solution will formulate in good time.

* * * * * *

Tia remained at Greyrivers, being taught by Master Harris. She enjoyed his enlightened instruction and how his experiences were similar to those who knew Christ Himself (with respect to their personal attachment to God).

She was reading one of the scrolls 'Wolf' Harris brought with him, when she asked, 'So you gave it all up just for Him?'

'*Take yeself up and follow Me,*' he paraphrased, 'And I did just that, and wanting for nothing. In the eyes and arms of God, everything is possible and everyone is looked after. I also get help from others who come to me, foodstuffs, wine and old bits of clothing, in exchange for instruction and baptism, if they choose to do so. I firmly feel I did well for the community, out in the sticks, as they say. Our Lord cares for us all.'

'I guess God does care, which was the point, I take it,' Tia surmised.

'He did not want His followers to worry about earthly matters, when a larger matter was at hand,' 'Wolf' Harris explained.

'The Kingdom of God, perchance?' *What a guess... duh!*

'Right you are, my dear. You catch on fast.'

'Only if the topic interests me. God was a big part of my scene back then, but what they did with and to Him now, is abominable. Those people just care about their own shit and not that of others,' she grimaced.

'Indeed not, from what I have witnessed, though I would not put it like that. When I lived in the desert, some of the people who came to me were Monos actually fleeing the pressure and oppression from their *own* communities.'

Tia got just a tad overexcited. 'So, there were others? Others who suffered like me, being preached to be one thing when they really were not?'

'Well, they were not oppressed by grandparents, per se, like you were, but let us just say, they had issues. The whole livelihood was hindering them and they wanted to choose a better path to God. Now, it is true that Jesus had failed initial expectations, but there were some who later appreciated His work and when it came down to it, turned to me for advice and guidance.'

'Sounds all too familiar,' she shook her head in disgust.

'Wolf' Harris looked kindly at her, 'I do not wish to pry, but maybe it will help you. Did you know your natural mother, at least? I am aware of what happened to Silardicus.'

'I knew her for only a too-few short years, if you know what I mean. I remember her saying to me, *I know where your father is*, but had never followed through with it. She was ill for most of her life, but more recently had succumbed to more difficult bouts... I do not know, it is just...,' she could not finish the sentence and buried her head in her arms.

He realised he touched a nerve and did not further the matter. He made a more tactful approach. 'What about this soldier, Coralanus? How do you really feel about him?'

Her eyes glimmered with hope at hearing his name. *Coralanus.* Her disposition changed and confidence breached through her insecure pallor.

'He means a lot to me; I feel the world for him and would ram a sword through it, if it allows me to keep such a gentleman next to my heart and body,' she exclaimed.

'But a soldier he kills the body, am I correct? I would think he would show no mercy in battle,' he argued.

'He may kill the body, sir, but my grandparents kill the soul.'

My grandparents kill the soul, she said... 'Wolf' Harris dwelled on her point. *And what a point it was...* His purpose in life was to save souls and he deemed hers was a very special one.

'Fine. I understand. So, it is not just a forlorn love-fascination with him, then. Certainly he is not just a carnal figure to you? He had helped you in need.'

'He got me out of *there*, and it was said that he would move mountains just to have me. He has a desire toward marriage. When we do so, would you officiate? I am sure Corry would appreciate that.'

'I am sure he would, Tia, though he has not committed to the faith. I will keep him in my prayers and see he comes to you shortly. He was very insistent when talking about you. I cannot help but notice that he refers to you as a *little bird*. Why is that?'

'Silly pet name brought on by a Mono name *they* gave me, which was Zipporah, meaning 'bird'.'

'Ah, an appropriate appellation that does not know what it is capable of.'

She laughed with him and he excused himself. He went to Greyrivers in his study and stood at the door, gently knocking.

'Am I interrupting you?'

Greyrivers, slightly dozing from reading endless paperwork, became startled, 'Wha--, wh--, oh, it's you. May I help?'

'Had you considered my proposition I made to you earlier. Tia has taken to my teaching well and I think I could benefit you and your workers, or slaves, as you prefer.'

Greyrivers had already affirmed the action in his mind. *What was good for the Emperor...*

'I agree to let you do your bit for my household and workers.'

'Splendid,' Master Harris proclaimed with excitement, 'You won't regret it, I can promise you that.'

He looked so pleased with himself, Greyrivers mused. *I guess living in the desert had given him a purpose, which was now coming to fruition.*

'I will allot one hour a day to you.'

'Yes, yes, that is fine. The young girl is catching on, as if the Mono's control of her had not stained into her consciousness. I believe there is hope and I want to give the others a chance, whilst I'm here.'

'The way things are going, I've observed, it will be a wonder if anyone would carry on with the old ways at all.'

Both laughed at one another and made arrangements for everyone on the estate to be instructed.

CHAPTER XIV

I was walking on my rounds with Eos on an assigned routine run, when many of our men were sent to quash another small outbreak of Mono resistance against our rule. The mini-uprising was centred near Lobim Lane, where previously, I had met Tia and I was alerted to the slammed shutters. *The Grass!* I was unsure as to what the grievance was, so Eos and I went in to investigate. We had an army of men along with us, so I felt safe.

In a short while, what I thought was rebellion against Rome, it was self-evident that the Monos *were* actively looking for Tia; being egged on by The Grass of Lobim Lane. *Oh, no!* I shook in my boots. This was a slight against carefully laid plans to remove my little bird from their horrid clutches, which would lead to a vile retribution by those grandparents. I rescued Tia, covertly, just before the slavers hit at that festival. I had thought it was discreet enough. *It seemed these Monos had eyes and ears everywhere.* The Grass had not seen the slavers take Tia away, but saw that someone else did... and that someone else was *me*. *At least, I knew Tia was elsewhere and they could not find her.*

Now that they were on the search, they saw my legion and viciously set upon them. The grandparents knew their charge was involved with a soldier and, to them, *all soldiers looked alike*. Eos and I did not want to get caught up with the melee and decided to pitch ourselves in a back alley along another street, out of the way. It was a risk, as I was still under confinement orders, but we had to take the chance. Our men could fight them anyway, so we snuck away. Anyhow, we needed to talk, and figure out what to do next.

'That Grass is unto us, and we've now confirmed that they are looking for your bird,' Eos exclaimed, exhausted.

'Don't worry, at least she's safe in the Valley, with Greyrivers,' I panted.

We breathed heavily, due to our flight, and I looked out to see if anyone was aroused by our presence. No one was... they were too busy fighting blindly with one another and our men.

Eos interjected, 'By the way, remember that night Nivien ordered your confinement, and I went out with the lads?'

'Yes,' I nodded.

'Well, I met a girl. She looks a bit like Tia, but taller... not by much. She's a Vespan. She's also up for their annual sacrifice this year.'

The Vespans... I recalled they were old school in Roman thought and belief, which by now would be a bit dated, and not to my tastes, but *who's to judge?* However, idea of this girl being this year's dead-girl-walking gave me much to ponder.

'Aside from height, what does she look like?'

'Slight build, pretty, intense blond hair that curls at the ends. If this lady is made up to look like your love, there are possibilities.' Eos growled lustfully at that point.

...if she was made up to look like her. I asked, 'Is there a formal ceremony or what?'

'I am unfamiliar with Vespan ways, but I believe it is a 'come as you are, do what you like' outfit. I think it best to visit the Temple of Vespa to seek this out. The way is not far. Just on the corner of Modde Lane.'

'I see,' I carried on thinking... gears and wet, lubricated cogs advanced into my psyche, providing me with a ready answer... *she could be a decoy... IF she was willing.*

It was her time to die anyway, and (to our knowledge) it did not matter *how* she died, as long as the deed was done.

The Monos were on the hunt and time was progressing. We needed to get past them. Eos and I checked out a corner to see the crowd thin out, but its remains were just as agitated. If they saw us, we would cop it... if Nivien saw us, we would get it. The fact that our story of Tia being captured by slavers was not holding up anymore, made me extremely worried and fearful. She was still in Mentis and if these people were resourceful enough, they could locate her in the Valley. *This could not happen.* Yet, as these people were blinded by their own hatred, Tia could be anyone, *and so could a soldier.*

We made our way carefully toward Modde Lane. The Temple was on the corner, just as Eos said.

'You like the Vespan, don't you, Eos?'

He gave me a huge, teasing grin.

I rolled my eyes, and wondered, 'How would you feel if you and her were 'caught' in a compromising position?'

'How do you mean?'

'You know,' I whispered my idea to him.

He reacted hotly, and concerned, eyes wide open, 'What do you have in mind, Corry?

'You know I would not put you in harm's way, but, this seems the only way.'

'What seems the only way?'

'I'll explain later.'

I hoped my plan would be accepted, for if this doesn't work, and we have to give Tia up, I might well run myself with sword and send all thoughts to Hades.

A short time later, a further multiple of tens had joined the irate crowd, giving it protestation with the agitated remains. The rumpus from earlier had not ceased after all, and the fresh injection of newcomers did not help matters. No one had dispersed, as hoped, and it was as if they were now holding a rally of some kind.

'She is still here,' I heard a few of them shout.

One of the Archevs shouted, 'Return her to us!'

'Fie upon her,' another went on, 'Soldier's slut!'

I got worried and dozens of flurries hit my system inside, wherein I felt helpless... nearly like my little bird under their strain. A soldier must *never* feel that way, especially if he was to quell the ongoing riots and demonstrations of the populace. My doubts had plummeted me further into a near-rash decision, but I had to hold on... just for a little bit longer.

'So where's that temple, Eos?'

'I'll take you, come on, before they see us,' he motioned me unto the next alley and we hurried on.

The vexation of the crowd was near boiling point, being wound up by the Grass and Tia's grandparents (who by this time, believed the mob that Tia was still around to find and catch). *I could never let that happen, ever!*

Everyone seemed too busy beating on everyone else and too blind to see anything in the distance. I figured we'd make it.

We headed toward Modde Lane. The Vespan Temple was towering in its being, though still typical of a *temple to the gods*. All in white stone, with several marble columns surrounding the front area. The public entrance was on the side, with a special entrance for the priestess and her twelve maiden assistants. The Vespans were similar to the Vestals, but differed in the sense that anyone could join it and one's virginity was optional. They allowed men inside the Temple, as long as they did not interact with the priestess and her maidens.

It was spartan enough, as a soldier's barracks would be, but with a woman's touch. A huge flame rose high above the dais, where Vespa's spirit would summon from within.

The twelve women were in the middle of worship, headed by an elder woman, known as the Bederah.

Eos and I filed toward a stone bench and stood with the rest of the small congregation present. We caught a minute taste of old-style pagan worship.

'And may the Goddess Vespa speed thee on they way,' the Bederah called out.

'And may Her eternal speed shine upon thy roads,' was the ready answer, with myself and Eos's voices as one.

'Vespa shall shine forth, with many headlights, to impair the darkness around us.'

'And may the darkness be impaired by Vespa's might and power.'

We sat down and, as I looked about me, I found all this *definitely* out-dated. *Could the new God be quickening upon me?* Eos smirked wildly when he saw the girl he met that night.

'You didn't say where you met her, Eos,' I said.

He gave me a look, then whispered, '*Knotted Ash.*'

'Get out of here,' I whispered hotly, 'No way!'

Eos kept to his mystery and continued to smile inanely. *That lucky beggar; I never get the breaks.* But as this girl is one of the twelve, we had to move carefully. His eye never left the girl. She was very beautiful (though I would prefer Tia to anyone else), with hair shining brighter than the Flame of Vespa. I recalled what he said regarding the lax attitude toward self-sacrifice and looked forward to meeting the Bederah.

I waited patiently and nervously for the *show* to be over, so I could speak to her. Once a gong had sounded and an elongated NOM sound had concluded, the twelve had retreated into the alcoves and the Bederah going into a small room. The precious little amount of congregants stood up, murmuring to one another in petty conversation, and leaving the site.

Eos made his move toward the alcoves, with myself following. We remained outside the door, out of respect for their meditation period. I found it awkward to imagine what she'd think of soldiers coming for public worship... yet, *everyone was welcome.* Our true purpose became evident in due time.

I knocked on the door, next to one of the alcoves.

'Just a moment,' a voice called out.

I waited, looking at Eos, who was still grinning, hoping he had found his match, as I had.

The door opened to reveal the Bederah; an older woman, with beautiful white hair, wearing a plain, monochrome robe. Her face seemed to be steeped in classical history.

She asked, 'What can I do for you gentleman?'

Eos and I looked at one another. I began, 'My friend had met one of your women the other night and he wanted to see her.'

'We don't usually allow people back here,' she stated.

I bit my lip and went on, 'This girl is due to be this year's sacrifice.'

'Ah, yes. Flo Pinjah. What do you want with her?'

This was getting complicated. 'Can we come in?' Eos blurted out.

'Certainly not! This is a holy sanctuary,' the Bederah protested.

'We are not interested in *that*,' I opposed, 'We need the girl for a mission.'

The Bederah was getting impatient and gave in. 'Come in and sit down. I will get Flo and we will get to the bottom of your request.' She huffed off to find her.

The room was rather claustrophobic to me, but it *was* meant for one person.

She returned with the girl and we began to discuss the matter. It was a sticky situation we were in and I had to think as fast as Mercury's feet.

'We need her to be a decoy for someone else,' I started.

'For whom? Your girlfriend?' The Bederah was getting rather snappy about this. *Oh dear!*

I blushed and Eos's need was getting greater. My need was far more worsened by the elder's potential to quash the Grand Plan.

'Yes,' I squirmed, having to tell the lady the truth, 'Her family is after her and if she is returned to them, there will be retribution upon her that I cannot bear to foresee. If Flo, who is due to be sacrificed, takes her place, then Vespa would be more than satisfied. Does it matter how the deed is done?'

'It is her responsibility to speed herself to the gods. There is preparation for this ritual called the Velocetos,' the Bederah confirmed.

'So, it is alright for us to have Flo?' Eos charged in with his denarii.

'Give Flo a week and come back. As her priestess, I cannot refuse. She will be prepared for your 'mission',' she turned to Flo, 'Is this arrangement to your satisfaction?'

'Yes, Bederah,' Flo agreed, turning to me, 'I will be happy to help save your girl.'

I smiled and gave her a kiss on the cheek. 'You do not know how much this means to me.'

'Well, then that settles it. See you in a week's time and Flo will be ready to do your bidding in the name of Vespa,' the Bederah shook my hand and Eos's and we left the room.

We went outside, past Modde Lane, away from the Temple. I felt tension in the air from the earlier perversion of people. Happily, most of them left the area. I let out a sigh of relief, as we headed toward our barracks. No one asked questions, as everyone there had been worn down by the day's infighting. Even dearest Nivien, with his scarlet of horror, had calmed down considerably, and had a very long snooze on his cot.

We were very damned lucky, indeed!

CHAPTER XV

An uneventful week passed. The rioting that had gone on earlier, had finally been quelled by us. Yet, those who started the bother had not stopped, but instead, held secret meetings in their homes and wandered through Mentis searching for my little bird.

Of course, we allowed them to carry on... it was all part of *my* plan against them; hence, the need for the sacrificial Vespan. Back at the barracks, I did some extra work, much to Nivien's satisfaction. I did not wish to incur the wrath of the Scarlet of Horror.

Eventually, my confinement was lifted and I was on the move once again. *There was much work to do.*

* * * * * *

Eos and I did our daily rounds in the town, policing a few streets in the area, as per usual. Luckily, one of our paths included a bit of coastline where Mobiah lived. We paid him another visit, expecting to be truly dampened by the experience.

We settled at a corner, with a stunning view overlooking the town. I noticed some burbling and bubbling about in the waters below. Naturally, we cleared away to give way to the huge entity that was Mobiah, who had emerged from his watery den.

'Ah, hello, it's you again,' the creature exclaimed.

Eos nodded respectfully, and I spoke, 'Yes, it is I.'

'So what brings you here, soldier?'

I stared out beyond the whale to see if that earlier view still remained... *it had not. Not with a whale in the way!*

'Much had elapsed since we last spoke, and I have a plan afoot,' I said, 'And will enact it soon.'

'Ummm....you got your little bird,' Mobiah guessed.

'She's now safe in the Valley, at the home of the Embalmer, which had been taken over by Greyrivers.'

'How long has she been out there? I trust the countryside would produce the calmness needed for her to heal.'

'Yea, she had been there long enough to find her beauty,' I swooned, thinking about her.

The whale smiled (or so it looked), 'You have been successful, then.'

'It has been a triumph, but not a complete victory,' my heart swelled in sudden agony, 'The Monos are actively looking for Tia.'

'Uh-oh,' he sighed.

'But, I have found someone to act as a decoy. She is a Vespan.'

'Oh, why a Vespan?'

'She's this year's sacrifice.'

'Ah yes, the 'come as you are; do as you like, as long as you do it' group.'

'That's the one. Eos, here, has the hots for this young maid. Don't you, lad?'

I turned to him to see his face buried in his hands in embarrassment.

The whale laughed. 'You're hooking your friend up with her? You know it cannot last.'

'We both know that. All that is needed is a soldier/girl couple that could be mistaken for myself and Tia.'

'I see. Bit crude, no?' Mobiah was sceptical.

'Nah, they don't know their right hand from their left... and neither knows what they are doing. They will never see past the long golden hair and the glitter of armour.

'No, I guess they would not,' he contemplated, 'They get very worked up about things; it makes them go blind.'

'That blindness will be to our advantage,' I confirmed.

'Well, good luck to you. When all this nonsense is past, I want to meet your little bird.'

'It will be an honour to do so,' I bowed before him.

Eos caught the ridiculousness of my action and cried, 'Corry!'

'What?'

'You're bowing to a whale,' he sniggered, 'I wonder what Nivien would think?' He continued to laugh.

'I do not give a flying squadron what Nivien thinks,' I hollered.

I then tsked to myself and returned to my conversation with Mobiah. 'I do look forward to seeing you again. One other thing, though...'

'Yes?'

'Do you have the capability of transport, as in a ship, you know, for speed?'

'So you want me to tow you and Tia in a getaway vehicle?'

'Ummm... not just Tia. There may be others, but I want to be certain that I get away from here with Tia.'

'I hope you find a stable enough ship that can withstand my wiggle.'

'Wiggle?' I got confused.

'It is the way I swim. Fish do not swim straight.'

Eos perked up. 'You're not a fish, you are a mammal.'

'Yes, but I still have my tail.'

Mobiah made his point by splashing us, good and proper.

He then asked me, 'Your idea of departure is based on Tia?'

'Yea, something like that.'

'Tell me, are you for Rome or the little bird?'

I blushed gravely, remembering the conversations I had with 'Wolf' Harris and Greyrivers regarding the same...

... but I did not have a choice... I loved the little bird, deeply.

'You just want Tia, Corry,' Eos remarked.

Mobiah reflected, 'I do not believe you are in it for the greater purpose.'

'You want the girl and get laid,' Eos added.

I turned to Eos, 'Well, don't you? What about that Vespan you're boning over?!'

'Hey, if you want to discuss your love lives...,' Mobiah paused.

'If you want to get me in with that Vespan, I would wish it to be more than just a fleeting moment,' Eos demanded.

My plan was more important to me than anything else. 'I will give you a night with her, alright?'

'That will do,' he smiled.

Mobiah took this in with a practical sense of humour. 'You two are absolutely wonderful men and lousy Roman soldiers.'

'Maybe there is more to life than being a Roman,' I interjected.

'Corry!' Eos was surprised.

'I wouldn't worry about it too much, lads. The Empire's packing it in anyway. High officials and soldiers are being recalled back to Rome.'

'We have never received orders of that kind,' I argued.

'It is taking its time to filter through the system and into the outer provinces.'

All my earlier doubts and self-questioning was coming quick to surface. The problem was, *I did not want them at this moment.* However, the heart spoke faster than the head.

'If that is the case, I'd rather pack it in myself, deal with Eos's problem, rid myself of the fucking Monos, grab Tia, and get the fuck out of this hellhole!'

'Now you're talking, Corry,' Eos smiled.

I exhaled, feeling the damp lining hidden under the armour. I was ready to shift myself away from this shit and get on with my life... whatever the consequence. *At this time, I did not care anymore.*

The whale came closer to me. 'You do what you must. I will help you move on and will see you again.'

'Thank you,' I whispered.

And the whale departed.

We looked like freaks-in-armour, and very soggy, indeed. The Scarlet of Horror would surely be upon us, if we did not clean up.

So we returned to the barracks to do just that. I later composed a note of leave to give to Nivien explaining the situation and I let him in on the plan I proposed. I also asked if he could partake in it and meet us with the legion and help during the confrontation. I would let him know when and where later.

* * * * * *

It wasn't long before Eos and I returned to the Vespan Temple to claim the sacrificial, Flo Pinjah, and help her along on the path... enacting the desperate plan I had to save Tia from that family.

We attended the public old-school worship service once more. My mind continued to doubt and question the now-dated ways and styles. I was still even questioning my position as a soldier of Rome, as horrid as that may be. I felt a betrayal of values (on my part) and it became clear to me that my life would steer along a *different* destiny. There was a further realisation that I, too, could use 'Wolf' Harris's instruction, help and guidance. I remembered my conversations with the fellow and my earlier consideration toward the new Christian faith was now turning into a firm conviction. *He earlier referred to that centurion...*

The service had come to its conclusion and I went to speak to the Bederah. I said an extra prayer, to make it alright and give me the hope I so longed for... the hope of having that little bird in *my* nest.

We waited at the door, as we previously did. The Bederah opened up.

'We are here for the girl,' I said impatiently.

'Yes. I know. Come in,' she rustled herself amongst the scrolls. 'You are aware she will have up to forty-eight hours to do the deed.'

'Alright,' I agreed. Eos stared at me with a craved look I had not seen before.

She went to fetch the girl. A few nail-biting, butterfly-turning-in-stomach moments passed by.

'Don't get too involved, Eos,' I warned, 'Remember, she is a decoy for my little bird.'

He pleaded, 'Can't we save her anyway, and get another person to cop it?'

'NO! We cannot back out now. Although this form of religion has had its heyday, we must respect its tenements.'

Eos pouted, glaring daggers at me.

'We still have the night with her,' I comforted him.

'I know, but...' He understood. *It's like a soldier's duty. It must be respected.*

Flo had emerged through the doorway with the older woman. She looked resplendent in a fine linen, lilac blue robe.

'I am ready to do your bidding,' she said quietly, consigned to her fate.

'May Vespa bless you upon your path.' The Bederah parted from us.

'Thank you very much,' I called out, taking Flo by the hand. I led her out of the Temple with Eos, into the passing evening sun.

'Corry, we cannot take her back to barracks,' Eos stated nervously.

'There is an inn near here, I am certain.' I had a scan around. 'Let us move along and see what we can find.'

'What about Nivien? You can't afford further confinement.'

'Don't worry, I left a message for him. We will be fine.'

I hoped we would be fine. I dreaded to imagine the Scarlet of Horror in action again.

In the meantime, we went to *The Knotted Ash* and ordered some drinks. We took to the private rooms downstairs to discuss the plan, and I caught a glimpse of Sans-Brys, who acknowledged me with a nod. I needed to speak to him, too.

We sat around a table and our drinks arrived. I took a sip, exhaled and began.

'You are aware you will serve us as a decoy for Tia.'

'Yes,' Flo said.

'Eos here wants to spend the night with you. Are you up for that? He really likes you.'

He widely grinned and she giggled. *This was no matchmaking, though.*

'I can entertain you both, if *you* are up for it,' she rang out.

WHAT?! My mind screamed. *Did she just invite me to join in?*

Eos looked shocked, but I was more reserved.

'I would be happy to spend an indulgence with you, ma'am,' I calmly spoke.

Eos was hesitant. 'What about Tia?'

'What about her? She's fine, and I need release. Anyway, I must rouse suspicion amongst the Monos to infer that I know where she is,' I thought aloud, 'I will find that Grass and it will take off from there.'

Flo asked, 'What will happen to me?'

'The Monos will catch you with the soldier, thinking it is myself and Tia, and put you into the custody of her grandparents.'

'So I will live as a Mono?'

'Worse. You will be spiritually hindered, sent to your room with a closed door, constantly criticised about a great many aspects of your person, and told you are a Mono, to the exclusion of anything and everything else. The other option is they stone you to death immediately, out of anger toward you and what was done to defy them.'

'I would rather take the stoning than live as a Mono,' she replied.

'I would too, but not under those circumstances,' I sympathised.

'Why are you longing to protect her?'

'I made a promise to her natural father, who was my commanding officer, to look after her. The family got in the way, and...'

'...stole the opportunity from you,' she finished the sentence.

'Yes, you can say that,' I sighed, thinking about all that happened. *It disgusted me.*

'She is safe elsewhere, I guess?'

I nodded. Eos stared at a painted mural of ecstasy. I looked around. There were many customers about and I did not want to give too much away... and I still needed to find Sans-Brys. Luckily, I heard loud applause and cat-calling from upstairs. The session was finished and I had a chance to catch him.

'Eos, you remain with Flo. I have a friend I need to meet up with,' I ordered.

'Sure thing, Corry,' Eos purred, looking eagerly at Flo, and kissed her.

I left them in their horny sunshine and went out to find Sans-Brys. I saw him file into his dressing room and I knocked on the door.

'Coralanus, what a surprise it is to see you. Come in,' he beckoned.

'Thank you,' I went in and sat down. He closed the door for needed privacy.

'It had been some time; how is that little bird of yours, um.. Tia?'

'Fine. I've sent her to the Valley, where she is living at the Embalmer's old villa. Greyrivers took it on some time ago.'

'Yes, you and your British slaves.'

'I know, I know. We get them from all places.'

'I noticed you had a girl with you. You said Tia was elsewhere.'

Was the planned deception working already? 'That is not Tia. The girl is a Vespan. She's this year's sacrifice and Tia's decoy.'

'Ah. You're going to pull one over on the Monos, are you?'

'They are so blind, they won't notice,' I assured.

'True, true. I remember what it was like. You are right to take advantage of it.'

'I search all sides, Sans-Brys.'

He looked out his window. Night was prominent. 'It is getting late. Are you staying anywhere in particular?'

'We were looking for an inn nearby...,' my voice trailed off.

'Don't worry. My house is your house. I live above these premises. I am sure I can make you accommodation.'

'Oh, would you? God, I couldn't impose.'

He waved dismissively, 'No imposition.' He then peered into my eyes. 'You said God.'

'Yes, what of it?'

'Are you resigning to the new faith? I know you dislike the Mono way.'

'It is a complicated mess I am in, Sans-Brys.' I then told him my doubts, my lack of belief in the old way, my wish to leave the Army and pursue my ever growing love for Tia.

'You need a break to help make up your mind,' he advised.

'I need Tia. Then, things will come together. I want to marry her.'

'You also want to be Christian,' Sans-Brys added.

He hit the nail on the head. *Oooh, that was a bad comparison. Damn!*

'You got me there. Are you done for the night?'

'I will be up shortly. Get your friends and meet me here in a few minutes.'

'I thank you from the bottom of my heart.'

'It is more from the bottom of your crotch, methinks, but never mind. I will see you soon.'

I got up and left the room. I went back downstairs and told Eos and Flo what transpired and that we could stay with Sans-Brys.

CHAPTER XVI

As planned, we spent the night with Sans-Brys. We did not have much with us, yet he was a gracious host. After a few more hours of a light meal and drinks, we bedded for the night, Sans-Brys slept on an ample sized sofa, whilst we took to his bed (once the sheets had been changed for us).

It turned out that Flo was well-versed in the art of love, as we were in the art of war. When both genres came together, words could not describe the experience. I allowed Eos his time with Flo, as I patiently waited. I went to the window and stared out. I noticed a small terrace, upon which I entered. I sat on a bench and took in the night air. Lights flickered in the township and I felt myself relax... *letting go of the armour...*

I was busy formulating a plan in my mind on how to grab the attention of the Monos to Flo. Of course, we knew she wasn't Tia (or Zipporah, to them), but I was secretly banking on the fact that their blindness could warp them into *thinking* it was her. I prayed to *whomever* about it. The flux I was in made me unsure of my god at this point. I found it all too overwhelming and further realised I no longer loved nor wanted Rome; *I loved Tia.*

The endless grunting and voices pulling at dangling string had made me think of Tia and how her development was coming along. I was sure by now, she had flowered into a massive garden, one of which that could compliment the Greyrivers home most honourably. *I could wait to have her... no need to rush these things.* There are other women one could thrust the sword into. Once I marry her though, the armour will be lifted and we shall leave this monstrous place.

My insides were suddenly becoming aroused. I got up and returned to the room to find Eos and Flo panting side by side with exhaustion. *Now, it was my turn.*

I removed the red tunic I wore, along with other bits about my person, and climbed atop the young girl. From my standpoint, she looked like a goddess.

I said to her, 'You are doing me a huge favour, don't you know?'

'Yes,' she answered back.

'It is not what we do now that counts.'

'I know.'

I propelled myself into her. 'I do not wish to proclaim upon your family tree. You will not live long enough to see the result.'

'I am aware,' she droned, knowing the inevitable.

I felt an aggression which usually stemmed from battle, but I refused to think of her as an enemy. She was good for purpose, which related to an earlier time when I last had a girl... but that was a long time ago, when I was a very young soldier... and too brash to care about anything else...

... but enough about that.

I got underway, with a renewed, lustful, pagan conviction. My thoughts were far from pure, and I honestly did not mind a fig for them...

Right now... right now...

... I had found the release sought for and fell asleep.

When morning came, I realised my condition and grabbed my tunic. Eos and Flo were intermingled in each other's arms.

I probably changed sides during sleep and they got together naturally. I gave Flo a kiss and whispered a quick 'thank you'. I went to seek Sans-Brys. I found him still snoozing on the sofa. He stirred, awaking in my presence, as I stood over him. I gave him some time to come to.

'Morning,' I said.

He slowly opened his eyes, responding instinctively, 'Morning.'

He let out a yawn and stretched. 'Hand me that chamber pot, will you?'

I did so and he went to a corner which had a privacy screen. He emerged and asked me if I needed it.

'Thank you kindly,' I took the pot from him and used the privacy screen, too. I emptied the contents out the adjacent window. A large splash was heard below, accompanied by a startled voice.

'Would you like some breakfast?' Sans-Brys offered.

'You are too kind, yes. Um...,' I thought about my uniform and needed a change of clothes. 'Do you have an extra tunic or something I could wear, instead of...,' I pointed to my military kit.

'You can have this. Doesn't fit me anyway, so you can keep it, if ye want.'

'Most kind.' I tried it on. *It did fit me.*

'Suits you, that does. What do you intend to do?'

'I need to arouse the Monos to our 'presence' so they could have that girl you saw and Tia will be forever safe.'

'I wish you much luck in your endeavour... but I would not take them for that stupid. They will eventually realise it is not her, even if they do kill her.'

'Could you help?'

'How?'

'Where would I find the fuckers at this time of day?'

'Oh, I guess they'd be at *their* morning services.'

'They have what??'

Sans-Brys looked pensive, rubbing his chin, 'If I remember correctly, they pray several times a day. So they'd be at their temple. If you want them to 'catch' your friend and the Vespan, I could kindly suggest you make your way out soon and wait in their vicinity, but well hidden. Personally, maybe wearing your uniform would be better. You can *pretend* you'd just been alerted to see what the fuss was about, or something of that nature. A disguise now would put you in a precarious situation.'

I thought about it, and for a dancer, the fellow made perfect sense. 'I'll keep the tunic, then and get my gear together,' I relented.

'That's the old boy. Now, you play soldier, set your friend and decoy up, make yourself scarce, then pounce on the scene, as though you had nothing to do with it. Then, could you fly away with that little bird of yours.'

That's it. Sans-Brys was right. 'Have you ever considered a different profession? You seem quite knowledgeable regarding matters of the world,' I suggested.

'I once was a professor at a local academy back in Gaul. I would like to return to it, as this constant dancing is doing my body in. I am not that young anymore,' he confessed.

'Would you return to Gaul?'

'If I had the power, money and passage, you bet I would!'

'I will be in touch with you later, when this shit clears up.'

'You know where to find me,' he grabbed a basket, 'Bread?'

'Don't mind if I do,' I accepted his offer and ate and drank a bit of wine.

I heard Flo and Eos stirring awake. I went in to greet them.

'Morning all,' I sang out. 'Sleep well?'

'Like a top, and still spinning,' Eos dreamily spoke, kissing Flo.

'We're having some breakfast, then we have to arouse the Monos,' I stated.

'Right.' Eos got into military mode and began his usual oblations.

I turned to Flo, 'You well?'

'Yes. I wish this done and over with,' she sighed, walking into the main room.

'Don't blame you. Hungry?' Sans-Brys motioned to the food. Flo went up to it and took a couple of grapes to eat.

'There is no appetite for death,' she said.

Sans-Brys and I looked at each other, knowing what will become of her.

Eos walked into the room, excited. 'Oooh, breakfast. May I?'

'Please,' Sans-Brys invited him.

'I do not know how to thank you enough for this,' I told Sans-Brys.

'Well, one good turn deserves another. How about that trip back to Gaul?'

'I think I could arrange something,' I pondered. *I got the whale, now I needed the ship to attach him to.*

Eos blurted out, 'Corry knows someone who can pilot a ship. We just need the ship.'

Sans-Brys got curious. 'Who?'

I blushed. 'Mobiah.'

'A sea captain friend of yours?'

'No, he's a talking whale,' Eos laughed.

Flo mouthed, 'Whale?'

The embarrassment was too much. 'Yes, I know a whale called Mobiah and he talks, alright?'

'Whatever you say,' Sans-Brys sniggered.

'He could help us,' I said.

'One thing at a time. Deal with your issue, then we will go from there.' Sans-Brys twitched his eyebrows, dubious of such a claim.

'You both ready for this. I know I am not, but as in a battle, we must proceed,' I ordered.

'Yes, sir,' Eos saluted, taking the girl.

'Farewell, Corry.' Sans-Brys gave me a hug. 'All the best to you.'

'I hope we can all be set free.' I gazed at him.

'Good luck.'

We left his private apartment to the public area and out the front door.

CHAPTER XVII

The time had arrived and I had to put my plan into action. Luckily, Sans-Brys knew a good place to do this. There was a temple nearby where the Monos had a morning prayer service, which (thankfully) lasted about an hour or so on a weekday. Today was Thursday. *Phew!* I remembered the day was named for the Norse god Thor, who wielded a hammer, as part of his kit. *Let us hope this proves correct, for I wanted to use that hammer and smash these fuckers myself!*

So, I sent another message to Nivien, via one of Sans-Brys's assistants, informing him as to where and when the plan is to unfold. I did not really care for an argument now.

I told Eos and Flo to remain with Sans-Brys and I stood watch, in my uniformed capacity, waiting for that unholy hour to terminate. As we roughly bade farewell to one another, we were as ready as a pie could be, and the conclusion of the Mono's services would lead to much solace in the long run. Everything I planned for, hinged on the timing of the moment. With already half-chewed fingertips, I stayed put, with nervous expectation. I stood, nearly helpless, wondering when Nivien would turn up, *for I could not face them alone.*

Suddenly, a touch of red caught the corner of my eye, as golden armour came towards me. It was Nivien, who marched with the best of the legion. Kirlus, Tontis, and Viamaturio were amongst the rest, and they were the ones I admired the most for their brawn, fighting spirit and a principled outlook, in respect to soldiering. They were here for *me* and I was greatly touched by their loyalty, though I was curious to see why Nivien, of all people, happily went along with this.

He came up to me, 'We're here, as you requested of us and off to save your bird.'

I could no longer think of Nivien as the Scarlet of Horror, though it was more in respect to his complexion when tempered. I was touched by his understanding.

'So you are moved by my desires upon her?'

Nivien squirmed, not impressed with himself that he 'gave in' to a request of a lesser officer. 'Well, not exactly, but I see you will not give up your fight for her. Anyway, orders came down to us and we've been recalled. As there is nothing further to fight for, we thought to support you. If a commotion does break out, all the better.'

I was still in shock. 'So you are willing to help my cause?'

He gave me a smile. 'We all will, Coralanus.'

He gave me a brotherly hug, which caused the men to titter a bit. Nivien hushed them up and they stood to attention.

I went off to get Eos and Flo outside and into position by a wall located in the She-atzah Square. As the hour wore on, I suggested they get a head-start and enjoy themselves before the hell broke loose. They began to kiss, and after a few moments, it got more intimate. *This will surely wind the Monos up into a delirium.*

Flo then gazed at me. 'Thank you,' she said, 'I will do my best for you.'

'As long as you give Eos your best, their anger shall lead them and you will suit the flying colours that await you. Good luck to you both,' I replied.

I walked away from them and hid around a corner. I noticed a sundial that reflected the near-closing of the hour in question.

I was sweating and thinking, nervously glancing at my second and the Vespan. *What a way to go.* I felt slightly jealous, but it was doomed from the start, which was the point of this whole foray. The pair's intimacy got more intense, as I noticed... well, I blushed at the prospect, and I figured to keep it to myself.

Nivien's men also hid from sight and waited for the progress to come; they, too, caught a sneak peek at Eos and Flo, who were constantly at it with one another.

The sundial hit the tenth hour and a Mono appeared, talking to someone from their group. *Shit, it was the Grass!* She was oblivious to all around her, until a sudden noise pierced the silence.

'Augghhhhhh!' Eos moaned.

I sniggered, knowing what *that* was.

'There they are,' the Grass shouted, running back inside to *tell-all* within.

The congregation then filed out wildly, heading toward Eos and Flo. *The claustrophics* (a local word meaning 'enclosed chaos') *had commenced.*

The Archevs (the grandparents of Tia), had come out as well, in their dull and unsophisticated glory, asking, 'Where is she?'

'There, with the soldier,' another Mono pointed out.

The crowd had moved fatally closer to the couple, like an ominous thundercloud in the sky. *The storm was about to hit and it promised to be a big one.*

I said a quick prayer to God, or whatever He was called... Jesus... *ah yes, that's it.* I appealed to His mercy to allow the satisfaction to continue...

... and it surely did.

Eos and Flo were indulging in their final love lust together, when suddenly Tia's grandmother, under the impression that Flo was her granddaughter, had lunged and pulled her away from Eos.

'Caught ya! Now, you will see what it means to defy us. You will never be freed from us and you will suffer heavily for this,' she hissed in anger, smacking her, pulling at her hair and pushing her through the crowd.

Flo took it all in, and accepted the ferocity placed upon her. She knew she was serving Vespa in all this, by giving in to the vengeful greed of the Mono way. *That alone made a good sacrifice.*

Eos was then brutally attacked by the crowd, due to his rude advances on 'their' girl. I stepped in, acting as if *fresh on the scene*, (remembering Sans-Brys' inference), and defending my second. Nivien and his men also appeared and rescued Eos from the thick of the crowd, giving him chance to make ready for a battle.

The crowd got incensed and cried out murder upon us. 'We hate you and we hate your rule over us. Get the hell out of our land!'

Nivien knew better than to rise to the bait and continued fighting them, with sword drawn and ready. We all used swords against them and we managed to take a few of the Monos out.

Flo, meanwhile, was taken by another group of Monos (who did not engage the soldiers), led by the Archevs, who placed her against a wall.

Red, eager eyes stared vehemently at her and dishonourable hands took rocks and began to stone her. It was an agreed-to fate, as discussed in an earlier, quieter hour.

'Begone, ye witch, you evil mite,' they taunted Flo, as more rocks and stones were hurled her way. She screamed as the concrete persistently pelted her body. One rock hit the top of her head, caving it in and causing her to fall into the mass of stones beneath her feet.

Oddly enough, even the Archevs had a hand in all this, continually winding the crowd up with heated, catastrophic passion. It was rather crude to think they should relish the death of a family member... *it certainly proved they did not really care about her well-being after all.*

The good thing was that they did not realise that they had the wrong girl *and* the wrong soldier.

I was in the thick of the brawl, battling sword against fist, killing some very demonic and cowardly men. However, one of them was clever enough to strike a blow at me twice, right in my eyes, as I staggered into unconsciousness...

It began as a massive fight, which soon turned into a riot in the streets of Mentis, concentrating at the Square, where a young lady had been killed. Stoned to death by the Monos, she was, as the soldiers defended one of their own, whom she was with, against the masses.

The High Priest, Ben-Oliviyay, appeared at the edge of the building at last, perusing all around him. He saw the resulting riot, done by the congregants he only just spoken to a moment ago. He was thoroughly disgusted and horrified that his people would cause such a public nuisance to themselves; they were usually a very calmly and secluded bunch.

When his eye caught sight of a pile of stones with a hand sticking out, Ben-Oliviyay closed his eyes, shaking his head in disbelief.

He then called out, 'Stop, my people, STOP! What in God's name are you doing? Is this what I have taught you?'

The Monos ceased their destructive activities, some even in mid-action, which for them was lifesaving... only to be dealt with later...

'Have I taught you people in vain? What caused you to do evil? What is the meaning here?' He motioned his hand towards the downed girl, whose hand was still proud of the concrete. He went over to pick up a couple of the larger rocks to identify the victim of this wild fling.

His eyes popped open when he realised he saw a face he'd never seen before. He then returned the stones to their place, out of respect.

He got up and further addressed the congregation. 'Was there a legitimate reason you had stoned an innocent child?

'That girl is NOT innocent. That is Zipporah, who we caught with a soldier. She is an evil person, a liar and a sneak,' the grandmother fumed, raising her hand to Ben-Oliviyay.

'An evil, sneaky liar, eh?' Ben-Oliviyay challenged. 'Then I ask you, Mrs Archev, is this your granddaughter, Zipporah?'

'YES IT IS!!!!!!!!!!!' The grandmother blew her violent attitude all around him.

The Grass supported the grandmother. 'That IS Zipporah Archev!'

Ben-Oliviyay was completely dismayed at their extreme behaviour and oblivious eye to reality.

'I must ask you to take a good look at this individual, who you've taken your so-called vengeance out on. I then demand an explanation as to why you had let loose your blazes upon her,' the Leader insisted.

The crowd murmured, and a voice cried, 'Check the fingers, check the fingers! The nails, the nails, find the nails!'

The grandfather, Mr Archev, bent down to check the girl's hand, knowing of the childhood accident that afflicted her, that was noticed by many of the congregants. Unfortunately for him, the girl's hand, although very dusty, had well-proportioned fingers, with the nails, beautifully intact and reasonably long. Doubt had crept in, so he raised the rocks to reveal the face.

It was a face he'd never seen before, either. He yelped from the revelation.

'THIS IS NOT HER,' he screamed, walking over to his wife (the grandmother), and firmly smacking her in the face. 'Why did you kill this girl? This is NOT Zipporah! Who the hell do you think you are? How dare you take away her natural family, which included OUR daughter, Susan, if you care to remember, and suffocate her with your form of child-rearing?!!! It is no wonder she hates us and, what's more, I DO NOT BLAME HER! You horrible woman. I am ashamed to be married to you!'

Mr Archev walked off in a huff, leaving his wife, the foul-mannered grandmother to contemplate her condition. A Roman soldier suddenly approached her, sword drawn...

Ben-Oliviyay had had enough and began to reconsider his position in the community. It was apparent that he decided then and there to reject them and pursue a new discourse on religious matters.

He certainly could not convince this populace...

'If this is your interpretation of all I have taught you, then I no longer want to remain your leader. I hereby resign and wipe my hands clean of you all. You can do what you want and answer to the fates.'

The crowd stared in disbelief as they saw their High Priest rip the clothes off his body and freeing himself of the religious regalia he'd worn, and sworn by, for years.

He then spat upon the discarded garments and metallic pieces. 'Do what ye want with them. Find yourselves another leader.'

Ben-Oliviyay had passionately walked away toward the soldiers, who by now, had finished their conflict with the rioters. The man had a presence about him which made everyone stand still in time.

He aimed his gait toward Nivien. 'Take me to Master Harris, please.'

After seeing a once-great man, reduced to someone clad in undergarments, Nivien wanted something first. 'Help me with Coralanus, then. He's been hurt.'

The two men brought the soldier Coralanus to a cart, to be returned to barracks. The favoured three, Kirlus, Tontis, and Viamaturio, pulled the cart on their own, taking their comrade to safety.

The crowd dispersed, still numb from recent events and without a leader. Ben-Oliviyay followed Nivien and his group back to the garrison. A couple of passers-by realised the girl beneath the rocks was a Vespan, and took her body to the Temple of Modde Lane.

CHAPTER XVIII

A few hours later, I came to. My head hurt continuously and I realised I was safe in my billeted bunk. I felt as if I had been washed in my own urine, yet still unclean.

A familiar face appeared unto me. It was my second and dear friend, Eos.

'Your plan worked, Corry,' he said, 'But, are you alright?'

'Yes,' I answered him. 'Christ, what happened?'

'Subscribing to the new faith, eh?' Eos tittered, as he brought me up to speed on the passing events of the Square. Then he added, 'I also saw the grandmother, you know.'

I perked up.

'I dispatched her on yours and Tia's behalf. I thought to give the last blow in the name of Silardicus and Coralanus,' he confessed, smiling.

I was dumbstruck. 'No way!'

'Yes, Corry. I delivered a parcel of a stroke. You were cast aside by a few punches near your eyes, so I trod upon the assumed path, to rid the world of that wretched grandmother,' he stated majestically.

I thought my eyes seemed a bit swollen. I lightly rubbed them and confirmed the same. 'I look a-shit, don't I?'

'Raccoon eyes, my friend,' Eos laughed.

I took this in good turn. 'At least you disposed of the grandmother. Tia will be pleased.'

'That is not all, Corry.'

He looked serious. Uh-oh. The curiosity was intoxicating...

'The grandfather had a row with the bitch wife and left her. That is when I slew her.'

'Looks like he saw sense.'

'There's more.'

I turned my head. 'More?'

Eos nodded. 'Their leader, Ben-Oliviyay has joined our side. He stripped himself in front of everyone, down to his nethers, and asked Nivien to take him to Master Harris.'

'A High Priest of the Monos wanting to meet with the desert rat, 'Wolf' Harris?'

Eos gazed intensely at me, affirming, *'Factum est ita.'*

There was silence between us. *When Eos spoke formally, he was serious.* I was completely shocked at how the plan turned out. The Archevs fell out with one another, leaving the grandmother defenceless against the sword of Eos Carmikulus. The Mono's prominent leader, Ben-Oliviyay, now taking up our standard, after bitterly rejecting the actions of his community and the community itself.

My God, this will be one for the history books!

* * * * * *

I wrote a letter to Tia, explaining my long absence (*well, it felt long!*) and describing the unusual events that transpired, from our confrontation with the Monos in the square, to my plan which saved Tia from getting ensnared again by her family, and the brutal, yet justified killing of her grandmother. I also included my intention to visit her. It was a lengthy correspondence, compared to the quick-button notes we used to send each other. Eos was sent out to deliver the message. I told him to remain at the villa until we arrived a few days later.

Nivien also had correspondence confirming the orders to withdraw from Mentis, this time from the new Governor, Clivetum, a Roman citizen (originally from Britannia) who challenged Claudiodufus' hold on the region. Nivien had acknowledged the recall in writing and planned to leave as soon as convenient. He wrote to the Governor explaining the dire circumstances, referring to the rioting that took place, the stoning of the Vespan and a vow that needed to be fulfilled by one of his tribunes (i.e., myself). He observed Roman power was slipping at this point and was relieved to hear of the end. He needed a ship to take us back, wherever.

In the meantime, Nivien arranged horse transport and we headed for the Valley, taking the newly notioned Ben-Oliviyay with us. I found it refreshing that such a great mind had seen beyond the limitations of the Mono lifestyle. He saw the error of his (*and their*) ways, and decided to follow an ancestor, who converted to Christianity a long time ago (but was never spoken about).

When we reached the villa, I saw the slave-force at work. They looked dishevelled, some stripped to the waist (due to the heat), and others panted from exhaustion of the day's labour.

'*Salve,*' I called out, waving. By now, I felt more familiar with these fellows, slaves, or not. *They were still human, dammit.*

Xan Woodes glanced up. 'Ah, hello there, soldier. Your girlfriend is by the porch. I think you will be pleased to see her.'

'*Gratias*,' I chirped, thanking him, as I galloped toward the villa. I saw Tia there, as Xan said she'd be, looking far more radiant than I'd ever imagined.

I raced to the post, where I hitched my horse, and Tia was already running to greet me. My heart leaped with excitement, as we embraced one another firmly and kissed.

'Corry, Corry,' she exclaimed.

'My little bird. It had been too long. I am deeply sorry for my delay.'

We hugged and kissed some more. Tia noticed something was amiss. 'What happened to your eyes?'

I figured my eyes had cleared up by now, but I had not noticed. 'That is what I came to tell you about.'

Eos and Nivien approached us. I introduced Tia to Nivien.

'So you're the cause of all the fuss and rioting about in town, and I had thought we had all been made redundant,' Nivien smiled, shaking her hand.

'I was unaware that I did cause fuss, and if I did, I apologise for the transgression.' She looked down at her feet submissively.

I did not like this. 'Tia, my love. It was not your fault your family led those around them to clamour for your blood. You are safe now, forever.'

'Corry,' she began to cry and held me.

Nivien realised all the fuss was true and we really did love one another. Eos made a face of acknowledgement.

'All that went on, sir, was for honour, ' he said to his superior.

'True to the very being,' Nivien responded.

Ben-Oliviyay came to us. He saw a familiar face... *but, not the one on the rocks.*

'Zipporah?'

Tia looked up hastily, confused. 'You?!'

'It's me, I'm afraid... yes,' he said nervously.

'My name is Tia. I have always been Tia since my natural father had me baptised as an infant. Master Harris told me so, cos he performed it on me.'

'I see. Well, I decided to change my name to...'

This was news.

She asked, 'To what?'

'I will call myself… Simon Oliviyay.'

'I think that sounds better,' Tia smiled.

'I also need to discuss a very sensitive matter, as I've come to a stern decision.'

Tia had a quizzical look on her face. 'You're having a mid-life crisis, aren't you?'

'Mid-life or not, it is a crisis. After I saw my very own congregation run rampant and turn our religion into a shambolic mockery, I resolved to change my life... to the way Jesus Christ preached.'

'Ah, so you wish to become Christian,' Eos figured out, 'Coralanus here has similar designs, don't you?'

My face reddened in embarrassment, but I faced up to my destiny. 'He's correct. I want to convert, too.'

'Looks like Master Harris will have a flock like no other,' Nivien noted.

'With a great mind such as yours, there will be endless conversation between you both,' Tia giggled.

Oliviyay smiled at her comment and thought that with *his* education, he should be a complementary match for the lone 'Wolf'.

Yet, there were other matters more immediate.

Nivien addressed Tia, 'Are you aware of what happened to your grandparents?'

'Corry, I mean, Coralanus had written to me, telling me about a riot, intense fighting and someone being killed in my stead...,' she struggled to recall anything further.

Eos stated, 'There was a girl who we had to have killed to make your family believe it was you. But please do not worry. It was a mutual agreement and she was due for sacrifice anyway.'

'Who was she? Did she look like me?'

I cleared my throat, 'She looked far better than you, but she was not my type. Eos was more keen on her than I was. The lady was a Vespan, of the old-school tradition.'

'She was a pagan, then,' Tia surmised.

'Yes, and willing to take your place, in order to save you, my little bird,' I continued.

'If she was more beautiful than I, and perfect in every way, then *how* could they think it was me?'

Oliviyay stepped into our chat. 'Inner blindness, ignorance and arrogance. It certainly was not what I taught them to be, although it did not hinder the eventual outcome.'

Tia was really stunned. 'So they really thought this girl was ME?'

We nodded.

'Even down to the hands?' Tia showed us the affliction her grandfather and other Monos had looked for on the girl that got stoned.

'When it was found the hands were not yours, the grandfather freaked out, had words with your grandmother, and left her. I thought divorce was in the air for them,' Oliviyay stated.

Eos carried on, 'There was an... *opportunity*. I took stock of the moment. The grandmother stood alone. Coralanus was knocked out and someone had to strike against her.'

'Furthermore, as my second, he did what was expected,' I remarked, 'And I deeply regret not dispensing that final act against her.'

There were no tears for Tia regarding the passing of the grandmother, but tears did flow for our loyalty to Tia and what she meant to me. She felt a profound relief at the news and ran to Eos, thanking him warmly.

Eos stared into her eyes, 'And I would do it all again, for your honour and the honour your father, the immortal General Silardicus.'

Master 'Wolf' Harris joined in at this point.

'You've come back,' he said to us. He then saw Oliviyay. 'I remember you. We had many an argument, back in the day.'

'I've changed radically since then and now need your help, as does this soldier, called Coral...,' Oliviyay tried to say my name, but could not pronounce it correctly.

'Call me Corry,' I said, 'Yes, I will need guidance too.'

'Wolf' Harris chortled, 'So you have fallen for the *Big One*, eh?'

I looked up at the sky, then to Master Harris. 'Yes, I have.'

'I am delighted to hear it. I have been instructing and baptising for a long time and it would an honour for more people join my flock.'

Our group muttered among themselves. There was more to tell, and Nivien asked for attention.

'We've all been instructed to leave Mentis, at our earliest convenience.'

I thought I'd heard this before, when Greyrivers emerged from inside to join us. 'Home?! You mean we can return to Britannia?'

Nivien turned to him. 'You did alright here, didn't you?'

'I suppose I did, but remember I had been taken here, by force, to be a slave. It was my efforts that freed me.'

'You won't be the only freeman around here. You have your group over there,' Nivien pointed at the British slaves, still working hard. 'It is in your power to free them and return to your home province. We're packing it in ourselves.'

'Shall I get them?' Greyrivers proposed.

'If you must,' Nivien sighed.

Tia turned to me, 'Corry, I want to take you up on your offer of marriage and I want Master Harris to perform it for us.'

I gathered her gently in my arms and brought her to him.

'Master Harris?'

The elder caught our attention. 'Yes?'

I asked, 'When you've given me your instruction and initiation, may you marry Tia to me?'

'I would love to,' the lone 'Wolf' beamed, 'You know, Tia's quite the disciple. Maybe she could instruct you. Anyone could instruct, if they are full of the Holy Spirit.'

Personally, I wanted Tia full of something else... *but that's another issue entirely.*

I smiled back, 'I believe I shall have better knowledge coming from you. Tia is a distraction to me, and a delicious one at best. You can educate me and Master Oliviyay together, if it makes it easier.'

'I think I could arrange that.'

Greyrivers returned with the silly beggars we called slaves and addressed them. 'General Nivien has orders for us to vacate this property. The Empire has fallen. You are going home, and you are going home freed men, by my power as your owner.'

Buckingham piped up, 'So we are to return to Britannia?'

'Once a ship is prepared for us, yes,' Greyrivers answered.

'Yeeeoooowwww,' the other slaves shouted in gleeful anticipation.

'Home to my wife and family,' Xan reminisced, sighing, 'I'd forgotten what it was like.'

Cateliffe felt suspicious, 'It'll be a bastard of a journey, though, wouldn't it?'

Eos spoke to Nivien, 'Coralanus has something to tell you in respect to this ship.'

Nivien questioned me, 'Coralanus?'

I knew what this meant. *It was bad enough telling Sans-Brys about it.*

'I have a friend who is willing to steer the ship for us and could make record time.'

'With us at the oars, we will make it home by tea-time... a month later, at least,' Xan replied.

I shook my head. 'No, faster than that.'

'There is not a single boat, ship, trireme, or polystyrene that could make it to Britannia any faster than good ol' man-power,' Nivien argued.

'This friend of mine is no *ordinary* seaman...,' my voice trailed off.

'Well, then, who is he?' Nivien was insistent in his Scarlet of Horror look. The rest of the group looked on with suspense.

'Mobiah,' I uttered.

'Who is...? Yes?!!!' Everyone in the group waited.

Eos relieved the group of the pressure. 'Mobiah is a talking whale who is willing to assist us. All we need is the ship. He is a very righteous creature, once you get to know him. Just mind the splashes, though.'

Everyone then turned to me. Oliviyay was aghast. 'You're putting our lives in the hands, I mean, fins, of a whale... that talks??! I know the story of Jonah, but this is most unnerving to me.'

'Know you such a creature, Corry,' Tia wondered.

The Scarlet of Horror was relentless. 'Do you mean that all the times you've been out on patrol, you've been talking to a whale?'

'I have met him on a few occasions,' I admitted, 'But I never shirked my duties.'

'I should hope not,' Nivien was livid.

'It's all over now, anyway,' I pouted.

'Yea, that it is, and furthermore, it is getting late. Anyone hungry?' Greyrivers invited, 'I know I am and you may all join me.'

The Scarlet of Horror turned a placid pink once more. 'Rather. I'd forgotten the time.'

'It is easy to forget the time when there is much in disarray,' Oliviyay observed.

Nivien turned to him. 'And we are in the thick of it, and now need to re-arrange ourselves.'

An hour or so later, our meal was ready, all hands preparing it; food, fruit, wine and chatter never before working in such a harmonious fashion.

CHAPTER XIX

Some weeks went by. Nivien, having now witnessed how much Tia meant to me, had granted me indefinite leave from the Army. Thus, I remained with her at Greyrivers. I spent most of the days receiving instruction and eventual baptism into the new faith from Master Harris. My fellow convert, Oliviyay, underwent the same as I did, but for him it took longer, as his ever-questioning nature interfered with the advice *to have faith*.

Once I was welcomed into the Christian religion, I made arrangements with 'Wolf' Harris to marry Tia. Tia, of course, had no family; we took care of *that*, yet I had her father's blessing of long ago... a blessing to which I strived to have fulfilled. This was why I longed for the little bird, swearing off *all* women, throughout my life... waiting, hoping and praying forever to have her. This was first and foremost on my mind, and I confess, to the exclusion of all else.

And at last, my time had come. Eos, naturally, would be my best man, and we asked Oliviyay to walk the dear girl in procession to a makeshift altar (as the ceremony was held at the Greyrivers villa). I was in my finest form, but only in that light-fitting tunic, courtesy of Sans-Brys. As I was on leave, Nivien thought it would be best not to sport me in the gear as a soldier. Tia looked lovely in a long white gown, adorned with some spiffy ornamentals.

'Wolf' Harris had us exchange vows in front of everyone present. The ceremony reflected the Christian way, so no sacrifices were made. Nivien was there, all the former British slaves, Clarence, Greyrivers, his wife and her servant, Eos, and Oliviyay. I even had the audacity to invite Sans-Brys; *after all he had done for us, I felt he deserved a place.*

Once our union was finalised, our match was celebrated by a lavish feast. The Valley boasted natural beauty, as well as bounty, which was taken full advantage of. There was much fruit, wine, cakes, bread, and fish.

Music was played and everyone danced into the late evening hours. It was great to have my little bird now known as Mrs Tia Coralanus. She thought it sounded noble. *I thought it suited her well.*

A messenger from the Governor's office filtered an urgent message into our festivities. Nivien paused to read the glad tidings it brought:

To General Nivien, 12th Legion of Silardicus
From Governor Clivetum, Harodd's Palace, Mentis

We have made a trireme available for you to facilitate your vacation from this territory of Mentis. Your destination is your choice, if it is not Rome. You have a month to quit this land.

We gathered around Nivien, who could hardly believe it. The confirmation was official.

'We are going home,' he beamed, hastily deciding to cast his lot with us.

The former slaves let out a yelp of joy and everyone else wept with the same sentiment. It looked like I had to pay Mobiah another visit, this time with Tia.

* * * * * *

Visiting the dear whale became easier, with that leave I was hereby granted. Tia and I went on this calling together and found that special place down the alley, where Mobiah resided.

Earlier, I warned Tia about his habit of splashing about everywhere, which (of course) can't be helped. It was an inevitable part of meeting such a creature.

We stood by, awaiting the predicted bubbling... which soon occurred after I'd exhaled an anxious breath. As the water took charge of me, it held me in its persistent grip.

'Hello, Corry,' Mobiah greeted me, 'I see you have charming company today.'

Proudly, I introduced Tia, at last, to the great creature.

'Ah, so this is the little bird with whom y'wish to fly away with,' he smiled.

'Hello,' Tia said, nervously.

I glanced at Tia, 'Don't be afraid, my love.'

'She looks certainly worth all the nonsense you put up with, just to get her,' he commented.

I then told the whale, 'She *was* worth all the fuss.'

Tia chimed, 'Is this the fellow who will bring us to a new place?'

'Yes, my dear. He will take us to one of our outer provinces.'

Mobiah asked, 'We had not agreed yet, Corry. You still need that ship.'

'And we have one,' I spoke, 'My superior had just gotten word from the Governor that we are to leave this place and go forth to wherever.'

'Wherever? That's a bit vague, no?'

'We have a month's time to leave and we were thinking of going to Britannia, with a quick stop along the Gallic coast.'

I could not forget my promise to Sans-Brys.

'Oooh,' Mobiah grimaced, 'That's a long way from here.'

'We have newly freed slaves that want to return to their families, and I want to make a better life for me. There is nothing for me here; there is nothing for me in Rome. I've no family. Tia has no family. We only have each other.'

The creature had an idea. 'I have some colleagues who may be able to assist me and circumvent the duration, and could control that wiggle of mine.'

I definitely hadn't forgotten about that! 'Who do you know can assist us?'

'For many years, I have swam these seas and met many a fellow sea creature of all kinds. The ones I have in mind are mermaids and mermen, collectively known as mercastes.'

'Mercastes?' Tia mouthed.

'They are half-casted sea people. Half-human, half-fish; thus, called mercastes. Makes it easier for identification,' Mobiah explained.

'So how will they help?' Now, I was getting cynical.

'They would push the rear of the vessel and steady it, as I steer up front,' he said.

'This is so exciting,' Tia squealed.

'Well, you let me know when you are leaving and I will have my team ready for you. With all the fish in the sea, it should make a reasonable voyage,' Mobiah replied.

'I will and look forward to seeing you,' I waved goodbye, as the whale's fin rose out of the water to do likewise.

Unfortunately, the result of this got us a right sodden-through. As it was a hot day, the experience was welcoming this time.

Tia attempted to jest with me. 'Your friend there would make an excellent priest.'

'Why?'

'Cos he's good at baptisms,' she laughed.

Ha-ha, very funny, my little bird!

We walked along the old streets where we (properly) first met, which was some time ago. There was silence everywhere. Even the dodgy area of Lobim Lane had a hushed-feel to it. I heard no door, shutter or window slam shut....

... and this silence sounded so good to me.

Later, we went into the barracks, and I asked Tia to wait outside. I needed to speak to Nivien about the departure and told him I wanted to bring another friend along.

Nivien stared at me. 'Who?'

'Sans-Brys, sir.'

'The dancer?'

'Yes. He helped us before the great riot and stoning took place. He gave us shelter for the night and he wishes to return to Gaul and his professorship.'

'Have you raised this with his owner? Remember, this friend of yours is a slave.'

'Surely, you can buy the owner off,' I scoffed.

'An army wage is meagre to buy back a slave, especially one of his quality.'

'We could always use force,' I suggested, pointing to my sword.

Nivien thought about it and sighed. 'Leave it to me. I cannot promise anything, but I will try my authority upon the owner to free your friend.'

I grinned and shook his hand. 'It would mean a lot to me, if you are able to do this.'

'No worries,' he paused. 'By the way, how's married life treating you?'

'Well worth the battle to achieve it, sir.'

'You have a heart warming passion, don't you?'

Now was my chance to tell him I wanted out. 'I have a confession to make, General.'

'Funny thing to say to me, you need that Harris fellow for that,' Nivien sniggered.

My tone got serious, and my eyes were pleading. 'I want to formally leave the army and return to Britannia with Tia, along with the rest.'

'My sentiment is with you, Coralanus. I do not want to lose you, but I see you've fought your battles well and won. You deserve the honoured victory, and I shall grant you permanent leave.'

'Maybe you can find your own little bird out there.'

Nivien's scarlet flag rose, ignoring the comment. 'I trust you will still require your 2-IC, Eos Carmikulus.'

'I want him to carry on as my second, yes.' I went on to another subject. 'The whale has been informed of our intention.'

'Oh? He will help us?'

'With assistants, he will.'

'What kind of assistants?' Nivien's brow raised.

'Mercastes that will control the ship from the rear. Mobiah will steer the front end.'

'Mercastes?'

'A race of half-human, half-fish people.'

Nivien's hand shot to his head. 'That's just what we need now. More mythology!'

'I was constantly told to have faith, sir, and as a newly baptised Christian, I will uphold that motto, even unto the ridiculous.'

'You keep to your opinion, and you will go far... although, how far is questionable.'

'I'm going back to the Valley. Let me know when we're due to leave,' I called.

'Will do. Take care of yourself, Coralanus. Love to Tia from me,' he stood, shaking my hand.

I left the room and went outside. Tia sat there, and when she saw me, she gave me an affectionate embrace.

CHAPTER XX

A fine day in June brought us to our departure from Mentis. Nivien's command of the legion had expired and he was now made redundant. The Legion itself was disbanded and many of its members had gone back to Rome. Others such as Nivien, Eos, myself and Tia decided to go to the outer province of Britannia with Greyrivers, his household and the newly-freed slaves. Even Governor Clivetum had joined us, as he started his life there and wished to return.

Greyrivers sold his estate to a local farmer, including the old villa and fruit orchards, for a fair sum. The local did very well, considering all the land he acquired, along with what went with it. Greyrivers left the furniture and other bits in the bargain, which he felt would help the farmer on his way. The farmer was most grateful, though he would have to hire his *own* labourers.

Tia and I headed for the harbour, where the trireme had waited for us. I needed to get my aquatic friend over here, so we broke rank to find him, running to find the alley of his domain.

'Mobiah,' I called out.

A moment passed and the familiar greeting met us both, as the whale appeared from beneath the surface.

'Hello! I guess you are here to tell me you are ready to leave.'

'I am. The ship is being loaded and boarded as we speak,' I replied.

'I'll be there. Shan't take too long. I need to gather up the mercastes. See you there.'

The whale disappeared and we returned to the ship.

Tia felt a bit of trepidation about the coming voyage. I gave her a reassuring hug.

'Don't worry, my little bird,' I said softly, 'Our nest is waiting for you in another land and we will be there soon enough.'

'Corry, I cannot wait to have you,' she cried, burying her face in my chest.

Her sentiments hit hard, as I felt anxious, too. 'I will do all to make you happy, and erase the past. We're going to a place where no one knows us, and will never know of our history. We can surely begin afresh... and I have faith Mobiah will get us there, as he promised.'

We carried on along the path, until we reached the harbour. There was a colossal harness attached to the trireme, made especially for Mobiah. The vessel looked sturdy enough to hold all of us, even with whale power in charge of it. I boarded the ship, Tia first, of course. We did not bring much, as we severed our ties to begin anew. Tia, though, had a small bag, which she kept with her. Greyrivers and his household packed quite a bit... it was good the cargo hold was large enough to take it all in.

And, what once belonged to me was returned to the Army.

A voice was heard above the din of preparation. Nivien lent over the side to see a late middle-aged woman.

'Yes?'

The lady asked, 'Room for one more?'

I glanced over the side, too. By Heaven, it was the Bederah! *I wondered what she was doing here.*

Nivien rolled his eyes. I approached him and whispered about my association with her.

'Alright, come aboard,' he granted.

I went straight up to her, recognising her from our previous meetings.

'Remember me?'

She turned to look, 'You're that soldier that entered my temple.'

I nodded.

'So you are leaving too?'

I told her about recent decisions I made and that I got happily married to the girl I wanted.

'I am pleased for you...um... I cannot recall your name.'

'Coralanus. And you?'

'Call me Wilmah.'

I smiled at her.

'The attendance at the Temple had been sparse in recent weeks, and a new faith had taken hold of most of my followers, it seems.'

'It did me, too. Even the leader of the Monos capitulated to the new regime.'

'No kidding,' she gasped, knowing of the strictness of the former Ben-Oliviyay. 'Well, the girls and I gave Flo a decent send-off and agreed to quit this and move on. This new religion of Christ seems fascinating to me and I want to learn more about it.'

'I know of such a man to help you on your way,' I held out my hand, encouraging her to follow.

I led her to one of the various cabins, where I found 'Wolf' Harris and Oliviyay discussing theology together. I introduced them to the pagan priestess. The two men were elated to find a new point of view to argue with and they welcomed the dear lady with open arms... literally, as they were taken in by her ancient beauty.

I left them to it and found Tia, when suddenly the vessel rocked a bit from the waves caused by my leviathan friend, Mobiah. She fell into my arms from the motion.

'I'm here, Corry, and these are the twelve mercastes who will assist me,' he announced.

'Good. I'll get you hooked up onto the harness and we will be ready to leave.' To Tia, I asked, 'You alright?'

'Yes, thank you,' she straightened herself up.

Nerves controlled a huge space in my stomach, as I raced to find Nivien, whom I felt made a perfect commander.

After I told Nivien the whale arrived, he ordered the former slaves onto the deck to aid with the harness. When they appeared, they looked up at the curious creature that loomed before them.

Buckingham panicked, 'Umm... what is... who is??!'

Nivien tried to explain, but not having met Mobiah, he, too, freaked out.

He began to stutter. 'Th--th--this is Mobiah?'

Luckily Eos was on hand to grab Nivien, as he nearly swooned into a faint.

'This is Mobiah, my General,' Eos said.

Nivien came to, partially. Xan Woodes was more helpful. 'I'm used to odd creatures like this. I was told stories of them long ago, as a child. Damn me if I would happen to meet one myself!'

The British lads secured the whale to the ship.

Clivetum went over to us, oblivious to more current circumstances. 'What is all this? Aren't you slaves supposed to be paddling?'

Xan told him of our arrangement with the while.

'Well, blow me down in a storm. This may prove to be a most interesting journey,' the Governor exclaimed.

The ship began to protrude from the pier and into open waters. A series of fins were violently pushing through the waters and away from Mentis for good.

Tia was waiting for me by the side. She found it most amusing to see non-humans in control of the seas. I held my arm around Tia, as she watched the fish in action.

'Sometimes, we must take a step back,' I observed.

Clivetum motioned myself and Tia over to him.

'There is something I think you should know about your family, my dear girl. I had my men do some background digging and I think you will be amazed at the results,' the Governor said.

'Yea,' she anticipated the news with bated breath.

He continued, 'I found that there was corruption in government, whereby they were letting people into our society without proper documentation. My predecessor, Claudiodufus, had accepted bribes during his long time in office. He allowed in outsiders, who claimed *they* were entitled to this (*so-called*) land of the Monos. This specific family of yours is not from these parts. They originated from our Germanic region of Empire. They created an illusion about their heritage and had *snuck-in*, assuming themselves into the Mono's faith a couple of generations ago for marital and settlement purposes. They fraudulently declared this tradition to be theirs, and they carried on to keep the pretence, until the rioting and stoning happened and we had to step in.'

I could hardly believe it. 'So they were not real Monos?!!'

'No, and Tia, it seemed, had suffered in vain and we lost a whopping great General, because of *them*,' Clivetum grimly revealed.

I sighed, shrugging the negativity off, like an animal drying out its fur. 'Anyway, life will be far better, now *they've* gone for good.' I gave Tia a hug. Eos and Nivien had joined us; Nivien finally having regained his wits.

'And good riddance to a place like this,' he grumbled, realising we had left the shore.

'Amen to that,' Eos agreed.

'Amen,' I hummed silently, staring out at the sky.

A familiar oblong face approached me.

'Good to see you, Coralanus.'

It was Sans-Brys. We embraced.

'I managed to buy him off his owner... with a huge discount,' Nivien said, indicating his sword.

I laughed, and felt gleeful.

Sans-Brys had other news... the suspense carried over from Clivetum's.

'As a footnote, since Ben-Oliviyay's departure, the Monos elected one of their own to lead them. He is a layman, don't know his name, but he is no different from the others, and, unfortunately for them, just as bad.'

'No one is as good as Oliviyay, as he now likes to be called,' Nivien stated.

'Ah, I see. Good on him,' Sans-Brys remarked.

'He's having a heated discussion with Master Harris and that pagan woman, who I just let aboard,' Nivien continued.

'That'll keep them busy for hours,' Eos chuckled.

'If the Monos are as blind as we had witnessed, I would not be surprised if there was any in-fighting, and eventual dispersal of the group,' I commented.

'That remains to be seen,' Sans-Brys imagined.

'And furthermore, it turns out that Tia's not one of *them* after all. That family was *fake*,' I announced.

'Well, what do you know?' Sans-Brys smiled, looking at Tia, 'You are free of them, at last!'

Tia smiled back, letting in all the Light she acquired at Greyrivers.

* * * * * *

The journey itself lasted a couple of weeks, when we made it to Britannia's dampened shores. Thanks to the whale and mercastes, we made excellent time, although some of our group succumbed to seasickness. It was pleasant enough, despite the shining seas and aggressive waves splashing more fiercely compared to Mobiah's playful bouts...

The three 'professors' comprising of Wilmah, Master Harris and Oliviyay enthusiastically carried on engaging theological questions and founded a church in the Whitfir region; the British folk had returned to their tribe, the Clubretts, where they reunited with their respective families. Greyrivers and his house carried on their lives, whilst Eos, Nivien, and Clivetum became comrades in their own right. Sans-Brys went on to Gaul, where he continued his professorship, as he intended.

And as for myself, Titus Clunos Coralanus... I had my little bird.

www.ingramcontent.com/pod-product-compliance
Lightning Source LLC
Chambersburg PA
CBHW021018120726
47905CB00009B/3066

9780995591967